Twelve Days in December

Twelve Days in December

Michele Paige Holmes

Mirror Press

Copyright © 2016 Michele Paige Holmes
Print edition
All rights reserved

No part of this book may be reproduced in any form whatsoever without prior written permission of the publisher, except in the case of brief passages embodied in critical reviews and articles. This novel is a work of fiction. The characters, names, incidents, places, and dialog are products of the author's imagination and are not to be construed as real.

Interior Design by Rachael Anderson
Edited by Cassidy Wadsworth and Lisa Shepherd
Cover design by Rachael Anderson

Cover Photo Credit: Lee Avison/Trigger Image
Cover Photo Copyright: Lee Avison
Winter Scene Photo: Shutterstock #158009457, Copyright Shutova Elena

Published by Mirror Press, LLC
ISBN-10: 1-941145-79-5
ISBN-13: 978-1-941145-79-1

Dear Reader,

The story you are about to read is centered around two characters from my novel, *Marrying Christopher*. If you have read that book, you will recognize the opening chapter of *Twelve Days in December* to be the same as chapter forty-four in *Marrying Christopher*, only told from Charlotte's point of view. If you are new to these characters, I hope you enjoy becoming acquainted with them. Beyond the opening chapter, this romance is entirely William's and Charlotte's as this is their story about the miracle of love, in a season when we recall miracles and share love with our fellow men the most.

Merry Christmas and Happy Reading!

Michele

Other Books by Michele Paige Holmes

Counting Stars
All the Stars in Heaven
My Lucky Stars
Captive Heart
A Timeless Romance Anthology: European Collection
Timeless Regency Collection: A Midwinter Ball
Between Heaven and Earth
(Power of the Matchmaker series)

Hearthfire Romance Series:
Saving Grace
Loving Helen
Marrying Christopher

CHAPTER 1

December 20, 1828
Vancer Mansion, New York

Charlotte Holbrook paused in the hall outside her sister's door, listening to the weeping coming from the other side.

"Oh dear." Charlotte bit her lip in apprehension as she glanced at Lady Cosgrove, standing beside her, a distinctive frown turning the older woman's normally pinched look even more severe.

"What now?" Lady Cosgrove muttered. She withdrew a key from her pocket and fit it into the lock. She opened the door, and Charlotte and the maid bearing Marsali's gown hurried to enter behind her.

Across the room Marsali sat crumpled on the floor, her arms and tear-stained face draped over the window seat.

"Fetch a cool cloth," Lady Cosgrove instructed the maid.

"I will be well enough," Marsali said, sniffing loudly.

"Your *face* will not be." Lady Cosgrove crossed the

1

room and pulled Marsali to her feet. "Look what you have done to yourself. And with but two hours until we must leave."

"What is it, Marsali? What is wrong?" Charlotte steered her away from Lady Cosgrove and over to the bed, where Marsali collapsed, face down, upon the coverlet and began sobbing anew.

Lady Cosgrove bustled about the room, readying Marsali's wedding outfit, as if nothing was amiss, while Charlotte stood watch over her sister and fretted. Tears like this were not an indication of pre-wedding nerves or uncertainty. These heart-wrenching sobs denoted deep sorrow and an as-yet-unhealed broken heart. Charlotte knew the sound well enough. She had cried out her own anguish many times in the months since Matthew's death. Losing a husband was excruciating—no matter how short a time one had been married.

Lady Cosgrove instructed the maid to leave, then sat beside Marsali on the bed. Charlotte sat on her other side, ready to rise to her sister's defense. She had been in favor of this wedding and thought Marsali had been extraordinarily blessed in earning Mr. William Vancer's favor so quickly. That each had suffered a loss and found comfort in the other seemed entirely logical. And that Mr. Vancer was one of New York's wealthiest businessmen and could provide for Marsali all she needed, indeed all she might ever desire, was most fortunate. Considering the hardships each sister had faced the past years, Charlotte had felt vastly relieved to know that Marsali, at least, would be well cared for.

But perhaps she had been wrong to push Marsali toward marriage so soon. After all, scarcely three months had passed since the shipwreck which had claimed both Marsali's husband and Lady Cosgrove's daughter, Lydia, who had also been Mr. Vancer's fiancée. Lady Cosgrove had brought Marsali with her to Mr. Vancer's home to recover, and from there a friendship and affection between Mr. Vancer and Marsali had blossomed quickly. Or so Charlotte had believed.

She is not recovered nor ready to move on. Charlotte read the misery in Marsali's expression as she rolled over and sat up, facing them. *But if she does not take this chance now, she is not likely to get another.* Charlotte understood the realities of a woman trying to survive in America on her own. She must encourage Marsali to avoid such trials.

"It will get better," Charlotte promised as she took Marsali's hand. "You simply haven't had enough time. I still miss Matthew and love him and think of him every day, but I have learned that I must move on and make a life for myself and Alec. You have been forced to that conclusion early; that is all."

Marsali nodded, though the look in her eyes said she did not agree.

"It seems ridiculous to think that you loved Mr. Thatcher enough to warrant all this." Lady Cosgrove waved her hand over the pile of soggy handkerchiefs next to Marsali. "You did not talk of love the day Lydia and I helped to get you ready to marry him. Why, you did not even know each other a full month. You have had twice as long to become acquainted with Mr. Vancer."

"But Christopher and I *understood* each other," Marsali said. "We had each come from difficult circumstances, and those had shaped us into the people we are, with similar dreams and goals. We did *love* each other."

Charlotte understood. She and Matthew had come together from England. Their trials there and aboard the ship together and starting over in Virginia had bound them together in a way that others who had not lived what they had could ever know.

"Well, you are not going to make a difficult circumstance for Mr. Vancer this morning," Lady Cosgrove huffed. "He stands to lose a fortune if the two of you do not marry."

"Christopher lost a fortune *by* marrying me," Marsali cried. "He gave me his only thing of value—his grandfather's ring—and he pledged at least two years of his life working to pay off my debt. There was nothing to be gained by his actions."

"Simply because there is something to be gained by Mr. Vancer's does not mean he isn't a good man." Charlotte had found in Mr. Vancer the kindest man. He had sent a carriage all the way to Virginia for her, so she and Marsali might at last be reunited. And he had not seemed at all bothered that Alec had come with her and could often be seen and heard exploring the halls of the mansion. Charlotte had had her hands full, keeping her fifteen-month-old son out of mischief since their arrival, so many were the wonders for him to get into. And on those few occasions she had not been quite fast enough, and Alec had broken something or made a mess, Mr. Vancer had not seemed upset in the least. He had shown them both only consideration and gentleness.

"He is fond of you and will treat you well," Charlotte said.

"I know." Marsali fell back, her dark hair spilling across the pillows as fresh tears spilled from her brown eyes, reminding Charlotte very much of herself, just a few months earlier.

Though she had not been afforded the luxury of a comfortable bed or much time to weep over her loss. Alec had needed tending, and they had both required food and a roof over their heads, and she was the only one left to see to those things.

As I am the only one here who can help Marsali through this grief.

"If only I could stop thinking of Christopher," Marsali said. "But I still dream of him most every night. And when I am awake I imagine sometimes that I see him places—once on the street when Mr. Vancer and I were out driving. I even thought I saw Christopher at the masquerade ball."

"Oh, Marsali." Charlotte's voice was full of empathy, not reprimand.

Lady Cosgrove let out a slow, heavy sigh, as if resigning herself to something. "You did see him at the ball," she admitted quietly.

"*What?*" Charlotte exclaimed.

Marsali pushed herself up on her elbows and stared at Lady Cosgrove. "What did you say?"

"The truth." Lady Cosgrove's usually straight posture was now hunched, and she looked discomfited. She cleared her throat. "I fear I have done a terrible, terrible thing."

"Only if you are lying now," Marsali said. "Please, tell me."

Lady Cosgrove would not meet her eye but inhaled deeply, as if gathering strength, then launched into a tale of deceit that Charlotte could scarcely believe.

Christopher is—alive? She brought a hand to her racing heart and could only imagine what Marsali had to be feeling. *If this is true, she* cannot *marry Mr. Vancer.*

"I knew I should miss your company if you left," Lady Cosgrove said to Marsali. "A woman my age does not easily make friends in new circles. But with you as his bride, it was possible that I might."

"So you kept Christopher from Marsali because you

wished to be her *friend*?" Charlotte's face screwed up in anger, and it was all she could do to refrain from shaking the woman.

"I don't understand," Marsali said. "*Is* Christopher alive? Was he here?"

Lady Cosgrove continued her explanation without answering either of them. "Later, I believed I was doing what was best for you . . . But now I fear I have ruined more than one life with my meddling."

Perhaps not. Charlotte read the hope in her sister's eyes. She decided to change tactics with Lady Cosgrove, reasoning that anger—no matter how justified—would not gain them anything. They needed Lady Cosgrove's cooperation and help if they were to find Christopher.

"It may not be too late to mend your mistake." Charlotte softened her voice, and she took Lady Cosgrove's hand and inquired about Christopher once more.

Lady Cosgrove sniffed and nodded slowly as she explained how Christopher had come to visit and she had told him Marsali was dead. "I was thinking of *you*," Lady Cosgrove insisted. "Mr. Thatcher had been seriously injured, and it appeared he would be lame for some time—perhaps permanently. I could see only a life of hardship ahead for you, if you remained his wife. I imagined you working to support not only yourself but him as well. But if you stayed with Mr. Vancer, you would never have to work, and you would have everything you ever wanted."

"I wanted Christopher," Marsali cried. "It was not your choice to make."

They continued their argument, Charlotte only half-listening and participating. *What is Marsali to do now? She is to be married to Mr. Vancer in two hours' time.* It was apparent Marsali had little thought of him at the moment, as she hurried about the room, donning her cloak and retrieving the wedding ring Christopher had given her. Charlotte stood and followed her, voicing concern over Marsali heading off to search for her husband alone.

"And what of Mr. Vancer, who fulfilled the debt?" Lady Cosgrove asked Marsali. "You would repay his kindness by abandoning him at this critical time?"

"We never should have *reached* this critical time had you been honest with us both," Marsali said, anger shaking her voice. "I regret that he will be hurt, but I *cannot* marry him now."

"He will lose his fortune *and* suffer public humiliation today," Lady Cosgrove murmured. "Oh! Whatever have I done?"

Marsali stepped around Charlotte and opened the door. "Somehow I think he would choose both over marriage to a woman who already has a living husband."

"Indeed I would." Mr. Vancer stood in the hall just outside her door, his brows pinched and a most stricken expression upon his face. "Forgive me. I did not mean to eavesdrop, but having heard my name mentioned, I paused outside your door and caught the end of your conversation. I gather you are going somewhere—and it is not to our wedding." He touched the edge of Marsali's cloak.

"My husband is alive," she said. "He has even been here—to your home—twice, without our knowledge. Lady Cosgrove at first told him I was dead and then later convinced him that I was better off with you."

"But you are not." Mr. Vancer cleared his throat uncomfortably.

"No," Marsali whispered. "I love him still. I must find him."

"Of course you must."

Mr. Vancer spoke with a great deal of understanding, and Charlotte felt her heart breaking for him. He had been so kind to Marsali, and they made such a handsome couple, his lighter hair and blue eyes a compliment to Marsali's darker coloring. *Dashingly handsome,* was how Charlotte had described him earlier. But now he just seemed distressingly sorrowful.

"This is quite the turn of events." He brought a hand to his temples and began rubbing. "In less than two hours we were to be at the church. Explaining to our guests shall be bad enough, but now I am left with only one week before the end of the year in which to find a wife. They are not easy to come by, you know." He gave a harsh laugh.

"I am so very sorry." Marsali touched his hand lightly. "I did not mean for this to happen. I never wanted to hurt you, and I shall find a way to repay every penny you have spent on me."

"You may have to," Mr. Vancer said, clearly jesting but with a trace of bitterness in his voice. "I have already made purchases and invested against the inheritance I was to receive. And now I will be unable to pay my creditors back."

"There is a possible solution," Lady Cosgrove suggested timidly.

Charlotte turned to look at her, astounded that she dared to even linger in their presence, let alone suggest anything—after all she had done to them both.

"I think I have had enough of your suggestions," Mr. Vancer said. "You accuse Marsali of repaying me poorly when you have betrayed the long-standing friendship of our families in such a manner."

"I did not intend to." Lady Cosgrove rose from her seat at the edge of the bed and crossed the room to the doorway. "When we arrived, I *did* believe Mr. Thatcher to be dead.

And when it was discovered that he was not, I did not know how to tell you—I was afraid for you and your predicament and concerned for Marsali and the otherwise harsh future ahead of her." Lady Cosgrove had crumpled a bit but straightened before adding, "And I truly believed that Mr. Thatcher had gone away for good."

"Clearly, he has not," Mr. Vancer said. "Nor would I, were Miss Abbott my wife." He blew out a long breath and leaned his head back, looking up, as if seeking inspiration.

"You can still marry today," Lady Cosgrove said. "Not Marsali, but Charlotte."

Me? Charlotte heard a gasp and wondered if it was her own.

"There is no doubt that *her* husband is deceased," Lady Cosgrove continued. "And she and Marsali are similar in appearance. Why, it is entirely possible that many in the congregation may not notice the difference."

"Aside from her *name,*" Mr. Vancer said, clearly exasperated.

Charlotte squeezed her eyes shut, humiliated at being thrust upon him thus.

"And," he continued, "I *would* rather lose a fortune than force . . . a woman to marriage."

She opened her eyes in time to catch him looking at her, assessing. *Asking?* In that brief instant she glimpsed his need—whether purely financial or something else beyond that she could not tell—and a vulnerability that reached her own, aching heart. *He is actually considering it.*

A tiny catch of hope, of possibility, stole her breath. Could this not be the answer to her own prayers? The very way she had been seeking to provide for herself and Alec? Her mind reached that conclusion before her heart had quite settled on it. "You would not—have to force me."

"Charlotte?" Marsali turned to her.

"I would not require much," Charlotte continued, looking past Marsali to keep her eyes locked with Mr. Vancer's. It was important he understand. "A roof over our heads and perhaps an education for Alec—when he is older. That is, of course, if you would not mind adopting a child in the bargain."

"I—would not mind." Mr. Vancer swallowed thickly. "Are you quite certain? We know very little of each other."

Beneath Charlotte's gown her heart beat wildly at the prospect of marrying a man she did not truly know. Marrying again. *Forgive me, Matthew. I am thinking of our son.*

"I know you have treated my sister kindly." Charlotte felt tears welling and fought to keep them at bay. She would have time enough later to both examine and cope with her emotions. But this here and now would come only once. If Marsali gaining Mr. Vancer's favor was good fortune, for Charlotte to earn his offer of marriage had to be direct heavenly intervention. "I have hope you would regard Alec and me the same."

"I would," Mr. Vancer said. "I will. I would be in your debt for so great a favor."

In my debt. It was entirely the other way around. He could save them from the life of privation and danger awaiting her at the plantation where she worked. *The very sort of life Lady Cosgrove was trying to save Marsali from.*

Marsali looked from one to the other, as if they'd each gone mad.

Perhaps I have, agreeing to marry a man I know so little of . . .

"It is all settled, then." Lady Cosgrove squared her shoulders. "Perhaps all will yet be well—for all concerned.

Come, Charlotte. You must be readied for your wedding. And, Mr. Vancer, I believe Miss Abbott is in need of a carriage."

"Yes—please," Marsali said, sounding focused once more.

"Godspeed, sister." Charlotte embraced her and added words of caution for her journey. "I shall give you the name of my employer, and perhaps you can take my place there. They should be happy to have a woman without a child tagging along as she does her work."

"Thank you," Marsali said. "I shall write to let you know what has become of me."

"You will do more than that," Mr. Vancer said. "You shall have an escort." His eyes strayed to Lady Cosgrove. "So your sister and I will not fear for your safety."

He does care for Marsali. Mr. Vancer had been reserved in his affection throughout the courtship, but Charlotte suspected it was only as a courtesy to Marsali. *He might have been starting to love her even. How will he regard me?*

"Thank you for your kindness and understanding," Marsali said. "If circumstances had been different . . ."

He smiled sadly. "But they are not, and you must go and find your Mr. Thatcher. I hope that when you do, he realizes how fortunate he is."

CHAPTER

After issuing a few orders, William left the women to take care of preparations and walked swiftly to the wing that held his private suite of rooms. He couldn't get there fast enough, or so it seemed, and by the time he reached the sanctuary of his bedroom, his fingers trembled then slipped on the knob when he tried to turn it.

Four times. This cannot be happening. His fingers managed to twist the knob, and on legs that felt weak, he entered the room. The door shut behind him, and he made straight for the chair near the window and the snifter of brandy on the side table. A thoughtful servant had delivered it earlier, saying it was for calming pre-wedding nerves, should William have any.

If he ever actually had a wedding, he might. *Four times. I must be cursed.* He sank heavily into the chair then reached for the glass. He brought it to his lips but at the last second thought the better of consuming even one drop of alcohol.

Charlotte had nearly two full hours in which to change her mind, and no doubt she would, though he couldn't help admiring the way she'd stepped in to save her sister, even if Charlotte would come to her senses and back down before all was said and done.

Brandy would certainly help ease the ache of disappointment he felt at the loss of his impending marriage to Marsali, but it would also impair his ability to handle the situation. He would need all his senses on alert and his wits about him in the upcoming hours, days, and weeks when the gossip columns and society pages would be filled with the news of his latest disaster. Imagining the headlines, he cringed.

American businessman William Vancer jilted at the altar yet again . . . Millionaire knows how to make money but can't seem to keep a bride. And worse—*Vancer Furs in trouble after overinvesting leaves Vancer unable to pay creditors.*

William leaned forward, his elbows braced on his knees and his head in his hands. What to do? Was it possible he might turn the story in his favor? After all, he was not only releasing Marsali from their betrothal, he'd vowed to do all he could to help her find her husband. Maybe New York would see his actions as self-sacrificing and noble, and he'd be well regarded for them.

But of course that didn't solve the problem of the money he'd been counting on. He already had a ship at sea, on its way around the horn, and he'd hired the guides and purchased equipment for an overland expedition to leave in early spring. He'd signed contracts and made down payments on additional land as well. If William didn't expand soon, John Astor's American Fur Company and Avery Hyde's Furrier Inc. would soon crowd him out and dominate the market.

They'll take from me what I've fought so hard to build.
He'd nearly lost it all before. Daphne Blackwood's heart-shaped face came unbidden to William's mind. He no longer regretted that she had chosen to marry Avery Hyde instead of him. Though he still held it against her that she'd waited so long to change her mind, jilting him the day of their wedding. He hadn't forgotten the humiliation he'd felt standing there alone at the church, waiting for her. He well remembered the pain that had engulfed him as he'd suffered through the awkward condolences and for months afterward had overheard the gossip surrounding his name.

Likely doesn't know how to treat a lady . . . Heard he had a fiancée in England who left him too . . . Must be harboring some terrible secret for Miss Blackwood to walk away from all that money.

But walked away she had, taking with her a vast knowledge of his business workings and a list of all his trappers, and his merchants both here and overseas, which she'd promptly shared with upstart Avery Hyde.

William would always regret being so open with her and the way he'd had to scrap to keep Vancer Furs going following their parting, but he could honestly say he was grateful he hadn't married her. That Hyde had so quickly made use of the information Daphne had shared with him only convinced William that Daphne and Avery deserved each other along with whatever misfortune their deceitfulness might eventually bring their way.

And what do I deserve? To be alone the rest of my life?

William was starting to think so. Alone was all right. It was tolerable, so long as he had his business to consume his time and passion. In spite of the trappers Hyde had stolen from him, in spite of the contracts Hyde had renegotiated out from under him, William had done more than keep

Vancer Furs alive. He'd seen it prosper greatly in recent years. Only Astor's American Fur Company did more business than he.

I might be second best, but I'm honest.

But honesty and good business ethics would not pay the bills. William supposed he oughtn't to have tested fate as he had, making plans and investing some of the money from his inheritance before he could legally claim it. *I should never plan on a life that is anything but solitary.*

He'd been mostly content with that arrangement—two broken engagements having soured him on the institution of marriage—until the news of an inheritance from his great uncle coincided with the letter from Lady Cosgrove last June. The condition of inheriting his uncle's estate—one he would sell and use the profits from—was that William be married. The letter from Lady Cosgrove, a longtime family friend, had told of her husband's death and hinted at the plight she and her daughter, Lydia, were facing. William had thought offering to marry Lydia was the perfect solution for both. His name and money would provide Lydia and her mother the security they needed, while Lydia would provide him with the wife *he* needed to claim his inheritance. And owing to her own precarious circumstances, it wasn't likely Lydia would break the engagement. He was safe.

Or so he'd believed. William sighed heavily, recalling the blow fate had once more dealt him when the *Amanda May*—the ship on which Lydia and her mother had sailed from England—had been struck by lightning and sunk just outside the New York Harbor.

So close, he remembered thinking as he'd read the shocking news in the morning paper and later learned of Lydia Cosgrove's death. He hadn't known Lydia at all, could scarcely recall meeting her in England years ago, when she was a child. *But still . . .* He knew he hadn't grieved her as he ought to. But he'd grieved what might have been. He had been eagerly anticipating meeting her. He'd hoped they would get along well.

And then came another hope, with Marsali.

William lifted his head and reached out, parting the curtain to peer down at the city below. He loved New York—the buildings, the bustle, the people. Marsali had not cared much for it. He'd realized that early on, but he'd believed she might change her mind after a while. Life was vibrant here and Marsali an effervescent young woman. It had seemed a perfect match.

His fiancée and Marsali's husband were two of the many who had perished on the *Amanda May*. And Marsali, too, was in a precarious situation, indentured to a Virginia plantation owner known for cruelty.

William recalled their first conversation over breakfast. He'd found Marsali's complete honesty a refreshing change from Daphne's falsehoods. He had liked Marsali at once and been only too pleased to pay her debts and hope that something might grow between them.

He had proceeded cautiously, never showing overt affection or allowing himself to develop any. That could come later, *after* their vows had been spoken.

Later should have been about an hour and a half from now, William mused as he withdrew his pocket watch.

Once more, dishonesty had robbed him of a bride. Lady Cosgrove's lies had nearly broken two hearts—Marsali's and her husband's. Fortunately, William had guarded his. Though this latest break of betrothal had the potential to collapse his business. He had little more than a week to secure a wife. *Twelve days until the year's end, and I must be married by then or lose the inheritance.*

In that event he would have to mortgage something to pay his creditors. It would be the beginning of a swift cycle downward, with Astor and Hyde waiting in the wings, only too eager to pounce on his misfortune.

So much hinged on the decision of the young woman in a room down the hall—a woman he knew very little about. He'd brought Charlotte here as a kindness to Marsali.

Will she now do the greatest of kindnesses to me?

He could not believe she would. An hour and a half was plenty of time for a woman to change her mind about marrying him. And given his past experience with fiancées, he had no doubt Charlotte would do just that.

CHAPTER

Charlotte stared at her reflection in the glass. The dress made for Marsali fit. *Another miracle.* Charlotte supposed she could credit her trim figure to the difficulties of the past few months. There had been neither enough hours to work nor enough food to eat in attempting to provide for herself and Alec.

Being a widow in America is not pleasant, secure, or happy. At least if you marry Mr. Vancer, you will have a chance at those. Charlotte recalled the very words she'd spoken to Marsali just a few weeks earlier, the night before the ball when her betrothal to Mr. Vancer was announced.

Now I must take my own advice. She fingered the cream lace of the beautiful gown. It would be nice to have pretty gowns once more, as she had when she was a girl, before Father died. But far more than that, she wanted to feel safe— for herself and Alec. She glanced at the bed where he was napping. *To never have to tell him that there is nothing to eat . . . to never have to leave him because I must work in the fields.* Her resolve grew stronger by the minute.

And as for not loving Mr. Vancer . . . What had she told Marsali? *Love is a choice. And you must choose to make it now, before it is too late and this opportunity is gone.*

But Marsali's situation had been different. She'd been married but a short while. *Matthew was my husband for nearly five years. We had a child together.* Marrying Mr. Vancer was one thing, but loving him would be another entirely.

Charlotte gathered the skirt of her gown and crossed the room, sitting beside Alec on the bed. Tenderly she brushed the curls back from his forehead. She *was* choosing love. Her love for her child compelled her to do this, to marry another when Matthew was less than a year in the grave.

Forgive me, she prayed again silently. And, as before when she had told Mr. Vancer she would take Marsali's place as his bride, Charlotte felt an overriding peace. Matthew would understand. He would forgive her.

But could she forgive herself?

She'd loved him since she was nineteen. Now, at twenty-four, she felt the passion of their youth, that time of falling in love with one another, slipping from her memory. Soon it would be gone altogether, replaced with the realities that were her life—unless she clung to them. And she could not allow herself to cling to memories of one husband once she pledged herself to another.

She must let go and choose a different kind of love, and she must do it today.

The peace she felt did not leave her but seemed to spread, engulfing her with a desperately needed tranquility.

Mindful that such serenity was precious, Charlotte stayed at her son's side, brushing her fingers lightly across his baby-soft cheek and imagining the possibilities ahead for him, the privileges he might have, growing up in this home.

With a whispered prayer of gratitude for the incredible turn of events, and a bittersweet smile on her face, she readied herself to speak new vows, to be a widow and single mother no more.

CHAPTER 4

William knocked on the guestroom door where Charlotte and her son had been staying. No answer came. He leaned closer to the door, listening for sound from the other side, but it was quiet within.

Gone already, then. Perhaps Charlotte had decided to accompany Marsali in the search for her husband. He had all but ordered Lady Cosgrove to go with Marsali as an escort. Family friend or no, he was furious with Lady Cosgrove and her lies that had and were going to cost him dearly. For both their sakes, it was best if she was gone from the house a good, long time.

The door before him began to open slowly. He was both surprised and pleased to see Charlotte on the other side. She placed a finger to her lips, then stepped back and beckoned him in.

"I could not call out to you to enter for fear I would wake Alec," she whispered, looking toward the bed where her son lay sleeping. If he misses his nap he gets most ornery."

"You haven't changed your mind then?" William asked, only just now taking in her ensemble. An elegant cream gown draped in layers of delicate lace fit close at her waist and hung with a full skirt near the floor. A matching lace band was woven through the curls of her hair, save those left to fall on either side of her face. And a pair of silk slippers peeked out from beneath her gown. He knew from listening to Lady Cosgrove that this was the wedding outfit that had been fashioned for Marsali.

"I have not changed my mind," Charlotte said, meeting his gaze directly, as she had in the hall earlier, when Lady Cosgrove had first proposed their match. "Do you wish me to?"

"No. Not at all." He shook his head, somewhat astounded at her directness and this potentially good news. *Though I dare not hope.*

"In that case, you should not be here, sir," she said, stepping closer, as if to usher him from the room. "Do you not know that it is ill luck to see a bride in her wedding gown before the ceremony?"

For some reason this made him chuckle, though there was nothing the least amusing about their situation. "Given the bad luck I have already had with brides, I cannot fear such superstition."

She frowned. "It is true, you have been most unfortunate. Twice now."

Twice. If she only knew. He supposed he should tell her that he had been previously betrothed a couple more times than that. *I will later. After—if—we are married today.*

"I came to see if you might consider going to the church now," he said. "I realize it is almost a full hour earlier than was planned, but with the change of brides, we will need to talk to the bishop, and there will be paperwork to fill out."

"Of course. I hadn't thought of that." Worry creased her brow a moment, causing her to look older than Marsali, and older than she likely was.

I don't even know her age, and we are to marry.

"Please give me a minute, and I'll get my cloak." She closed the door, practically on him, leaving him standing in the hall alone once more.

I don't know her age or much of anything about her—beyond what Marsali has shared with me. Which was likely more than she had shared about him with Charlotte. *We are the both of us mad to do this,* he concluded.

A moment later Charlotte reappeared in the doorway, a coarse brown, homespun cloak covering her dress. He noted that she looked no less pretty in the worn garment than she had in the wedding gown and silently agreed with Lady Cosgrove that Charlotte and Marsali did look a great deal alike. Perhaps those in the congregation would not notice that he had acquired a different bride. *At first.* But at the wedding breakfast after there would be explanations to give.

The least of my worries.

She glanced back at the bed where her son slept. "I think it would be best to leave him here while we go to the church. If we wake him early, he will cry for an hour."

"We can send Ellen up to sit with him and stay with him when he wakes," William suggested, recalling that the little boy had seemed to take to Ellen, more than some of the other maids he had interacted with.

"Yes, please," Charlotte said. "That would be best."

He held out his arm, she placed her hand lightly upon it, and they were off, with a quick stop to advise the housekeeper to send Ellen to watch over young Alec.

I will need to employ a nanny, William thought absently as they left the house. *And later a governess.* He would supply any sort of tutor Charlotte desired for her son, if only she went through with this today.

The brief carriage ride to the church was mostly silent, each busy with their own thoughts. He would have paid far more than a penny for hers but found himself too fearful to ask what she was thinking. *Will she refuse to get out of the carriage when we arrive? Or will I be waiting at the front of the church alone when she changes her mind?* He was not certain he could live through such a scenario again, though if that did happen, at least this time his heart would not be injured. He had learned to guard it well after Daphne. And watching Charlotte's calm, almost serene expression as she stared out the window, he had the feeling she had learned to guard hers also.

William wondered what her husband had been like. *Is she thinking of him now? How could she not be?* He suddenly wanted nothing more than to distract her from whatever sorrowful reflections she must be having. *How could they be anything other?*

The carriage turned the corner to the eastern side of St. John's Park. The trees lining the walk were bare now, dusted with a light layer of snow that had fallen the night before. "In summer this is a very popular spot for walking," he said, disrupting the silence in the carriage. "We could stroll there if you like. When the weather is warmer," he added, feeling unexpectedly foolish. It was a little late to be thinking of courting his bride now. Like all else that should have happened prior to this day, that would have to wait until after they were married.

"I would like that very much," Charlotte said and bestowed a kindly smile upon him. "Alec would like it too.

He enjoys being out of doors. Oh, is that the church?" She leaned in toward the window, attempting a better view.

"Yes. St. John's Chapel. Quite a fine building."

"I can see that." Her smile broadened.

"It cost an absurd amount of money. The organ alone was over $5,000. It came from Philadelphia."

Charlotte clasped her hands together. "I had no idea that America had such buildings as this. I can't wait to see the inside. The outside is perfectly grand."

William looked out his window as well, following her gaze from the Corinthian columns up to the double-height portico, topped by a tower that rose more than 200 feet. He'd been one of the men invited on an exclusive tour of the building when it had neared completion. The architecture had so impressed him, along with the added value the church brought to the upscale neighborhood, that William had easily agreed to put it at the top of his yearly donation list. He hoped the bishop would remember that today.

"I wish my mother was here—to see me wed in such a fine place and wearing a beautiful gown. And marrying a kind man." Her eyes flickered briefly to his before she turned her face, and a shy smile, away again. "She would be pleased."

He was pleased at Charlotte's assessment of the situation and felt his hope grow brighter. *Perhaps she won't change her mind.*

Now he had only to change the bishop's. Thankfully they were not in England, where a couple had to post banns. But still there would need to be new paperwork and, no doubt, money exchanged to accomplish that quickly.

The carriage stopped before the church, and they alighted. The steps had the same dusting of snow on them as the trees, so William put his arm around Charlotte's waist lest she slip. Given his poor luck with brides, he was taking absolutely no chances on anything happening to her. At least anything he could control. They reached the top step without incident and paused, turning to face her.

"I must ask you just once more. Are you *quite* certain you wish to go through with this?" It was the last thing he wished to say, but past experience bade him to. *Better she change her mind now than an hour from now when the pews are full and the organ is playing.*

"Are *you* quite certain?" Charlotte said, turning the question back to him. "You act almost as if you expect me to change my mind."

I do. "It is simply that I do not wish to force you to something you may regret later. You have not even had one day to reflect on your decision."

"I have had five months to reflect on it," she said. "Of necessity, I knew I must marry again. That it is to a man I know to be both kind and generous has brought an enormous amount of peace to my mind and heart. But you, also, must be certain."

On impulse he took her gloved hand in his, brought it to his lips, and kissed it. "Thank you, Charlotte. You cannot know the calm your reassurance brings to me. Once I begin something, I never change course, I can promise you that. Now let us go in."

He led her inside, watching from the corner of his eye as she took in the equally stunning interior with its towering side columns and sweeping arches. "I imagine you had opportunity to visit similarly grand churches in England," he said.

"Not England so much, but in France, yes. I have many fond memories of both the countryside and the cities."

"I return to England and the Continent every few years.

Perhaps you would like to accompany me on such a trip sometime?"

"Oh, yes." Her eyes lit up at the possibility, but in the next second her face fell. "Though I am not at all certain I would be able to survive another crossing."

It was his turn to smile. "Your accommodations would be considerably better than the last time. You came over in steerage, did you not?" He recalled Marsali telling him of her sister's near-death experience and felt suddenly grateful that Charlotte had survived that trip to be with him at this moment.

She nodded. "A memory I do not wish to revisit."

"Then we shall not," he agreed. They walked to the head of the chapel, and he escorted her through a side door and hall that led to Bishop Lewis's office. They met with him there, and all was accomplished with much more order and efficiency than William would have believed likely. At the end of their meeting, when Bishop Lewis shook Charlotte's hand with an exuberance that matched his unusually jovial countenance, William realized he had Charlotte to credit for their good fortune in getting through the particulars and paperwork with such ease.

She is a pleasant woman to be around, he noted happily. Marsali had not been unpleasant, but neither had she been wholly happy. He did not understand how Charlotte could be either, having lost her husband as she had, but she seemed far more resigned to, and at peace with, the idea of a new future than her sister had been. Bishop Lewis had taken to her at once, and upon learning that she was a widow with a small child, he had all but commended William for his good choice in providing for those in need.

William returned to the chapel to take his place at the front, while Charlotte waited at the side door. She would join him after all the guests were seated and the organ had played an interlude. Leaving her for even one minute started his nerves again, and he began to feel physically ill as he stood alone at the head of the pews.

He glanced over to the door and was surprised to see that Charlotte had opened it. She stood slightly back from the doorway so that she would not be visible to most, but clearly to him. He sent her a grateful smile, though she could not know what the simplicity of her action meant to him. So long as he could see her, he was safe. *I will be married today.*

He kept his gaze focused on her and noted once more how beautiful she looked in the cream gown. Her dark hair curled prettily around her face, and her hands clasped and unclasped in front of her, the only sign of nerves he had yet to note from her. She did not seem to be a woman given to blushing, perhaps owing to the fact that she had been married before.

William thought on this a moment, wondering how that might affect their marriage. According to Marsali, Charlotte's marriage had been a love match, one that had begun when she was quite young. But something between then and now had turned Charlotte quite sensible, enough so that she would readily agree to this marriage of convenience for them both.

Motherhood, he supposed. Wasn't it an innate quality in women that they would do whatever it took to protect their children? If that was true, he supposed he had young Alec to thank for his mother's being here today. William would have to do right by the child and make sure he was well provided for and educated.

He had enjoyed having the little boy running around the house. It brought a life to the place that had been missing, and William found he rather liked the idea of having more children to fill his vast home someday. He'd grown up in England, with a houseful of brothers, and he missed that. *I will have a wife and family of my own to share with my brothers the next time we meet.* Imagining himself introducing Charlotte and her son to his mother brought a feeling of comfort and pride, and William realized the situation was improving by the moment. To have gone from despair to near contentment and even pleasant anticipation for his future in the space of two hours seemed a miracle. *The day is full of them.*

At last the congregation was seated, the pews full of his business associates and friends, the elite of this city and a few who had come from farther away. *My friends.* Except that many were not, but were simply associates. The nature of his business demanded that he be acquainted with a great number of people, but it also meant he was close to none. Not since his relationship with Daphne had he allowed himself to truly trust or get too close to anyone. He had hoped that might change with Marsali. It would be nice to have one person in whom he could confide, one he felt would always be on his side no matter what.

His gaze locked on Charlotte's as she began to move toward him, walking carefully to match the music from the organ. It was too soon to know if she might be that one. For now, that she had agreed to be his wife was enough.

She took her place at his side, her gaze never wavering. Her expression was neither solemn nor happy, but somewhere in between, where his own emotions lay also. Bishop Lewis announced the reason they were gathered, then asked the required question of those in attendance, if there be any who objected to the marriage. William held his breath, believing this to be the last hurdle. When there was no response, he sighed, perhaps a bit too loudly; Charlotte looked up at him, a knowing smile upon her face.

He took her hand and held it, enjoying the feeling and once more overwhelmed with gratitude that she stood at his side. *How differently this day might have been.* That she had spared him extreme difficulties and potential disaster could not be overstated.

Bishop Lewis blessed them and read from scripture the importance of marriage. When he came to the line about the procreation of children, William kept his gaze straight ahead, though he wondered what Charlotte was thinking. He would like children of his own someday. But that could come later, well after they had come to know one another better.

Bishop Lewis continued. "Marriage was ordained for mutual society, help, and comfort—both in prosperity and adversity."

Help and comfort. That was what this marriage was based on. And if it was in scripture, then what he'd done— marrying Charlotte essentially to save his business—could not be so bad, could it? He intended to do his part as well, to comfort and help her and her son in any manner possible. *I will make up for my less than noble intentions,* he silently vowed.

When it came time for speaking the words, his voice was strong. Hers was equally sure, though he caught the quivering of her chin and the unmistakable glisten of unshed tears in her eyes when she promised to love him and cleave unto him and none other. He felt a sudden wish to comfort her, to enfold her in his embrace and promise that he would never take advantage of that promise or her in any way. Another man had loved her truly and loved her first, and William knew he must always respect that.

"I now pronounce you husband and wife." Bishop Lewis's grin spread nearly ear to ear.

Blessed relief washed over William, and the gratitude he

felt for Charlotte grew even more as he watched her brave smile and noted her blinking fast to keep her tears at bay. *This cost her.* No matter that she had said she was prepared for it; marrying again had cost her.

I will do everything I can to make it worth that cost. He could not make her stop loving her first husband, nor would that be right. But he could ease the worries and burdens she had borne since his passing. William could see she was comfortable and warm and safe; he could afford to buy her the nicest gowns and take her to France or anywhere else she desired. He would do all that and more, for she had truly saved him.

Not just his business, but him. *If she had not married me today, I should never have married at all.* Instinctively he knew losing Marsali would have been too much for him to ever try again. Charlotte had saved him from himself, from the lonely existence that had been his for so long. And someday, in years to come, God willing, she would assure that his line went on, that he had children and grandchildren to bless his life.

He owed her the moon, if that's what she wanted. *And the sun and the stars as well.* As they made their way down the aisle, hand in hand, amid the well-wishers, William could not recall having ever felt so happy before, nor more filled with purpose. The world seemed alive with possibility. All because of the woman beside him.

CHAPTER 5

"How do you feel?" Charlotte's new husband asked a question she did not wish to answer. Yet she could be nothing less than truthful with him. She turned her face from the window to look at Mr. Vancer seated across from her in the carriage.

"Exhausted," she said. "I had not realized that there would be so many people, so many faces and names to remember." They had gone directly from the church to the wedding breakfast, hosted by William's friends, the Fitzgeralds. It seemed the whole of the congregation had come, and the breakfast had stretched well past noon, a three-hour-long celebration wherein she had eaten very little but had been introduced to and spoken with what felt like hundreds of people.

Such an event should have been a good distraction to her tender emotions, but the constant congratulations and reminder that she had just married again had kept her on edge the entire time, fearful she might lose control and burst into tears at any minute. *And that would never do.* Only the thought of the embarrassment and anguish this would cause to Mr. Vancer had allowed her to keep her brave face as she mingled and greeted their guests. But oh, how she wished for the peace she had felt up until the very minute when she'd had to pledge her love to a man other than Matthew.

She had prayed his forgiveness too many times today to even think it again. What was done was done, and it had been the right thing to do. Hadn't it? Charlotte hated the doubts plaguing her even this minute.

"I am sorry I did not warn you about that," William said contritely. "The breakfast was the last thought in my mind this morning."

"That is understandable," Charlotte said with a tired smile. "And your friends are too kind, especially the Fitzgeralds. I liked them immensely. I promise to be better company in the future."

"You were fine company," he assured her, sounding genuine in his compliment. "I daresay there were a few men there today who were jealous of my good fortune."

Jealous because you had to marry your fiancée's older, widowed sister at the last minute when the woman you really cared for discovered her first husband to still be living? Doubtful. But Charlotte kept her peace on the matter. By and far those in attendance had been understanding and gracious when hearing of the circumstances that led to the last-minute change of brides. She'd been able to spot at once, those women who'd been overjoyed with such a juicy story to gossip about. But so long as she and Mr. Vancer—William, she must call him now—got along in the future, she did not see that there would be much to continue to gossip about.

Charlotte determined that it should be that way. She

and her husband would get on well, in spite of such an unusual and awkward beginning. Marriages had been arranged for centuries; and while they might be lacking the love she and Matthew had known, she believed that she and William could be good friends.

We can help and comfort and support one another as Bishop Lewis instructed.

It appeared that William intended to begin that immediately, as he scooted forward on his seat, rose, then turned around so that he was seated beside her instead of across from her as he had been.

"You are practically falling asleep," he noted. "Rest your head against me and close your eyes until we are home."

Home. What a lovely word. So long it had been since she'd felt as if she'd had one. All through her marriage to Matthew, and even before that, while staying at her aunt's house in Manchester, Charlotte had not felt as if she had a home. Always they had been guests or employees of someone else. Not since her family had left France had she known the sense of security that having a home meant.

William's arm came awkwardly around her, as if he was not quite certain how to make good on his offer, or if, on second thought, it was an entirely good idea. Charlotte wasn't certain it was either, but she could not deny that closing her eyes and resting sounded divine. So she scooted closer to him of necessity and leaned her head against his side. Gradually she felt the weight of his arm descend across her shoulder and arm, its warmth comforting.

She closed her eyes and sighed with contentment, giving into the need to be held for just a few minutes. So long it had been since anyone, aside from Alec, had shown her affection. To be cared for, just a little, returned some of the peace she had felt earlier.

This is right and good. Her eyes drooped, and she gave into sleep.

What seemed a minute later they were home. Mr. Vancer's voice was soft in her ear.

"Would you like me to carry you into the house?"

That woke her. Charlotte sat up quickly, her heart beating a panicked staccato as she realized her proximity to her new husband and his own, rather rapidly beating heart.

"No. Thank you." Where would he have carried her? To his room or hers? She couldn't think of that yet, of any intimacy beyond what they had just shared. And she prayed he would not either. "I should go check on Alec. He may be wondering what has become of me."

"Of course." Mr. Vancer withdrew his arm and straightened, putting as much distance between them as possible on the seat. "I meant to tell you—to ask, that is." He paused, seeming to search for the right words. "Marsali and I were to take a wedding trip through the end of the year. We had planned to go to Philadelphia and to see some of the other countryside, weather permitting, of course. You and I might still go, if you would like. I've allotted these last twelve days of December for the trip. Or, perhaps, with your son to care for, you would prefer not to travel?"

Charlotte definitely preferred not to travel, and not simply because that would mean leaving Alec. Mr. Vancer's house was grand, with plenty of space and bedrooms and the possibility that she might retain her own. But an inn in Philadelphia would likely prove an entirely different arrangement, one she was not at all ready for. "Might we stay home?" she asked. "It *would* be difficult to be away from Alec so long."

"I understand," Mr. Vancer said, his tone indiscernible and his expression unreadable in the low light of the carriage. "You two can get settled in, and there is always plenty of work for me to do at the office."

"There is not much settling in to be done beyond that which we have already accomplished," she said. An idea began to blossom through her haze of exhaustion. "What if you were to—would you consider still taking your twelve days in December off from your work?"

"You wish me to travel alone?" He sounded apprehensive, wary, and she hurried to explain.

"Not at all. I wish you to stay at home with us—with Alec and me. So he might become better acquainted, more familiar with you. You will be the only father he is to know. He is too young to remember Matthew." Her voice quavered at the last.

Relief eased the lines of Mr. Vancer's face. "I would be most happy to remain at home with you. And who is to say that we cannot take some day outings. It is the season of festivities, after all."

"Yes," Charlotte agreed, not feeling very festive at all, at the mention and thought of Matthew.

As if he knew the direction of her thoughts, Mr. Vancer took her hand in his. "This time will also allow you and me to become better acquainted. If it would not be too painful for you, I would like you to tell me about your first husband."

The tears that had been threatening all afternoon surfaced once more. "I am not certain that would be wise."

"I feel it not only wise, but necessary," Mr. Vancer said. "He is a part of your life, a part of you, the woman I should very much like to know." He released her hand, then used his own to brush a tear from her cheek. "But wait until you are ready. We have time enough—even beyond our twelve days, the first of which is nearly gone. Shall we go inside?"

She nodded, not trusting herself to do more than that. He knocked on the door of the carriage, and it was opened at once by a footman waiting outside in the cold. Charlotte wondered how long he had been there and how much of their dialogue had been overheard.

Mr. Vancer stepped down and waved the footman away, then turned to hold his hand out to her once more. She took it and noted that he did not let go, but kept hold of her as they made their way up the steps and into the house.

Just inside, it seemed that every servant had gathered in the foyer to greet them. Mr. Vancer paused just inside the doors. Looking most pleased, he announced, "May I present to you the new Mrs. Vancer, your mistress."

Cheers and applause erupted at this announcement, and Charlotte was overcome with another wave of well wishers.

"Bless you," the butler said as he shook her hand heartily. "It's a good thing you have done."

"Praises be. Finally," said Mrs. Duff, the housekeeper, going so far as to take Charlotte in an embrace before stepping back and giving a hasty curtsy. "We're all pleased as punch, ma'am."

"As am I." Mr. Vancer leaned close and dropped a kiss on the top of Charlotte's head. "Welcome home."

CHAPTER 6

December 21

Charlotte awoke early as was her custom, washed and dressed herself and Alec, then hurried below to the breakfast room. She had learned since her arrival several weeks before that Mr. Vancer—William, she reminded herself yet again—dined each morning at eight-thirty. It was difficult to think that yesterday morning the two of them had chatted amiably about the day to come, neither realizing that it was to be *their* day.

But the silver band on her finger confirmed that she had not dreamed yesterday's events. Marsali and Lady Cosgrove were gone; only she and Alec and William—along with an army of servants—remained at home.

How long will it take for this place to feel like home? Charlotte wondered as she carried Alec down the winding staircase. The house she had grown up in had been fine, but not nearly so grand as this. And now, in some measure, this one belonged to her.

"Good morning." She greeted the maid assigned to take Alec to the kitchen for his meal. It had been a change for them both, this eating separately, and often Charlotte made it a point to take her lunch with him in their room. But for now, the arrangement of dining alone with William had best be observed. They all had adjusting to do, and any changes she wished to implement would require both time and patience.

With a quick kiss to Alec's cheek and a promise that he would be given a cup of milk, she handed him off, then continued on her way to the breakfast room, where she found only two places set out—the one at which William was already seated, and the one directly to his right.

"Pleasant morning," he said upon seeing her.

"It is," she agreed. "Did you see all the snow that fell in the night?"

"Indeed." He rose and came around to assist with her chair.

Charlotte wondered at the absence of servants, then decided they had probably been asked to stay away, so the two of them might converse in private.

"I thought, since your boy likes the out of doors, that we might take a sleigh ride today, while there is still snow enough for it."

My boy. "Oh yes, please. Alec would love that."

"And you? Would you enjoy it as well?" William asked.

"If we are bundled warmly, yes." She had had enough of being cold the past few winters to last her the rest of her life.

"I shall set the cook to preparing potatoes or stones or some such warmth directly after breakfast," he promised.

Charlotte began to serve herself from the various dishes on the table, all the while pondering on his choice of words regarding Alec, and also the question William had asked of her in the carriage the night before. *There is no easy way to broach these topics. I shall simply have to be forthright.*

She took a bite of a biscuit spread generously with jam for fortification. "I would appreciate it very much if you would not refer to Alec as 'my boy.'" She looked carefully at William so as to judge how he took her words. "Henceforth, he is *ours*. I realize that affection for him may not come quickly, and it may not feel natural, but I plead with you to try to treat him as your own. He needs a father—now and even more so when he grows older."

William dabbed his napkin to his mouth before responding to her request. "I am honored that you feel thusly," he said, meeting her gaze. "And part of me, selfish though that part is, feels grateful that Alec is so young and will know only me as his father." His mouth twisted in apology. "As we have been entirely truthful with each other to this point, I would hope that we might continue, however many of my flaws and shortcomings that may reveal."

"I would imagine that your feelings on the matter are natural," Charlotte said, trying to think of how she would feel if it was he who had been previously married and had brought a child to their union. *Nervous*, she decided and realized she had, in some ways, an unfair advantage, having been wed before.

"I will do my best to do right by Alec," William promised. "And I hope to do so in a way his father would approve of."

He spoke with a tender sincerity, and his eyes held such hope of approval that Charlotte could not help but give it. She ·reached her hand out to him, patting his briefly in thanks. This earned her a reticent smile, and she withdrew her hand, also feeling inexplicably shy. They had touched frequently throughout the day yesterday, holding hands, brushing shoulders—actions expected of a newlywed couple. He had even had his arm around her in the carriage. *And that kiss on my head in front of the whole household.* But whatever familiarity they had achieved yesterday had somehow vanished.

I ought to feel grateful. Instead Charlotte sighed inwardly at the thought of starting all over again. Distance from one another was certainly a safer way to go about living, but if she was truthful with herself, she had to admit that she had enjoyed the comfort William's nearness and touch had brought. But perhaps he had not enjoyed it.

He is likely still thinking of Marsali. As should I be. Imagining how she would feel if she were to learn that Matthew still lived, Charlotte felt a wistful joy for her sister. *Be happy, Marsali. Be happy for both of us.*

And I shall do my best to be content and grateful—and attentive. She and William had the next eleven days to devote to their marriage, to decipher how they were to act as husband and wife.

The snowfall and sleigh ride proved nothing but providential. William directed the driver to take them to St. John's park once more, where they rode around the entire park, admiring the trees outlined with snow and icicles.

Alec squirmed to get out, so William called the driver to halt the team, and when they had stopped he jumped down into the snowdrift that came nearly to his knee.

"Come here, little man," William called, holding his hands out to the toddler. To his great surprise the child came willingly, practically falling into William's arms. Trudging slowly, William walked him to the grassy area of the park and set Alec down in snow less deep.

He squatted down closer to the child's height, then scooped up a ball of snow and began compacting it. "This is called snow," he told Alec. "And it's great fun, if you know how to use it."

"Ball," the little boy said, pointing to the creation in William's hands.

"Yes, snowball. And balls are for throwing." He pulled back his arm and lobbed it in a high arc at the sleigh, only to discover that Charlotte was no longer there. Or perhaps she was crouching on the seat. He told himself to remain calm, as he'd had to repeatedly throughout the day yesterday, whenever she had strayed from his side. Foolishly, he had believed that once married, his feelings of insecurity would disappear. She'd kept her promise to marry him, and all would be well. Except that he kept imagining her leaving. Vows or not, she might still change her mind about being his wife. As he'd feared she had last night when she had suggested he take the time he had planned off from work, though there was to be no wedding trip.

He'd imagined she would take the opportunity to leave while he traveled alone. How relieved he'd been to be wrong.

William stood, hoping to see into the sleigh, when something cold hit him squarely in the back of the head.

"Balls are for throwing, are they?"

He turned around and found Charlotte standing behind him, two additional snowballs balanced in her hands and a youthful, mischievous smile upon her lips. William stared at her for several seconds, transfixed at this change from the serious woman he'd had at his side yesterday. Her cheeks were rosy with cold, her eyes sparkling, and her lips . . .

Abruptly he pulled his thoughts from her mouth.

He held his hands up in surrender before quickly leaning down to swoop up Alec as a shield. "A good lesson to learn and learn young, my son, is that there is nothing wrong with surrender, especially where a woman is concerned."

Alec giggled at this or perhaps at the snow he was busily squishing between his mittened hands. These he brought forward and squished William's cheeks, shoving snow into his ear in the process.

William gave a playful shout, though his ear felt frozen, and set Alec back on the ground. Rubbing his ear and shaking his head sideways, he tried to remove the excess snow.

"Here. Let me." Charlotte dropped her snowballs and came to his rescue, even tugging off her own gloves in the effort. Her fingers brushed lightly across his stubbled cheeks, causing him to wish he'd shaved today. But when she touched his ear and her fingers tickled against the back of his neck he began wishing other things entirely and finally—out of desperation—removed her hand and held onto it, so she could touch him no more.

Is she purposely trying to drive me to distraction? She'd been married before and had to know what her touch could do to a man. But her smile was innocent.

"All better?" she asked.

That depended on what she was referring to. The cold was gone from his ear, but other things were starting to heat up, and he wasn't certain that either of them were ready for that yet.

"Yes, thank you." He released her and stepped back, putting distance between them and trying to remind himself that at this time yesterday he'd barely considered the prospect of marrying her at all.

It's too soon to feel anything for her. Even physical attraction. She is a mother, for heaven's sake!

William focused on that, on admiring her way with

Alec, the rest of the morning as they frolicked in the snow, building a lopsided snowman and lying on the ground to make snow angels. He'd been shocked when she suggested that, and for a split second worried that someone else might come along and see them on the ground, flailing their arms and legs and think they'd both lost their minds—or that he'd married a woman mad as hops.

But he'd very quickly decided he did not care. Daphne would certainly never have played in the snow with him. Neither, he imagined, would any of the women living in the mansions surrounding the park. But his wife was different. In her homespun cloak—he must remember to have a new one made for her—she didn't seem to care what others thought. A quality William decidedly appreciated.

He reached down, grasped her hands, and pulled her up from her last, and best, "angel," then looked down on it with her.

"Perfect," he said, wrapping his arm about her, while his other reached for Alec before the boy could step into the print and ruin it.

And though William had meant Charlotte's creation in the snow, in that moment he felt the same could be said of his life and his new little family.

CHAPTER 7

December 22

Charlotte meant to lie down for just a few minutes with Alec to get him to sleep for the night, but her eyelids drooped quickly, and a drowsy contentedness came over her as she snuggled beside her son.

What a whirlwind few days it had been. First the wedding, then their outing in the snow, and today William had taken her shopping, purchasing for her more hats and gloves and cloaks and gowns than she had ever dreamed of owning. She had tried protesting that it was too much, that she didn't possibly need so many clothes. But every time, he had silenced her with a finger to her lips or a quick kiss on the bridge of her nose.

"Allow me to spoil you this way. I am enjoying this. I've waited a long time to have a wife to take shopping."

She had finally ceased her protestations and enjoyed the excursion, though a part of her still felt guilty. After they had finished shopping they had taken tea with the Fitzgeralds, and then William had thoughtfully gone home so they might bring Alec to accompany them on a drive around the city.

William had shown them the wharf—to Alec's great delight. He loved the tall ships and had strained to get out of her arms and closer to one. William had also shown her the Park Theatre and promised to take her to a play or an opera soon.

All in all a delightful day, and Charlotte almost felt the need to pinch herself to believe it was real. It still seemed odd not to be rising early to carry firewood or start laundry or head for the fields. Living like this, without a care or worry for how she would provide for Alec, was going to take some getting used to.

I must do something to thank William, to show my gratitude for all he has done for us, was her last thought before drifting off to a peaceful sleep.

William knocked quietly on Charlotte's door, and when she did not answer, he reasoned it was all right to push it open a bit more, the door having already been ajar. He had grown fond of her company these past few days, and he had hoped she might join him for a game of chess or reading in the library after she put Alec to bed.

He felt both disappointment and a surge of tenderness when he saw that she had fallen asleep beside her son.

Unbidden, he stepped farther into the room, feeling drawn toward them, wanting somehow to reassure himself that they were both well. *This is what it feels like to be married, to have a family,* he realized with no small shock. *To care for someone so that they consume your every waking thought, to worry over their welfare.* He had only ever experienced those feelings with regards to his business and was surprised at the ease and intensity with which they had transferred to Charlotte and her son.

Our son, she had insisted. Already William could tell that would be no problem for either him or Alec. The little boy was endearing and brought a happiness to the house it had never known before. *I want to fill it with children,* William thought once more, then gazed upon his sleeping wife and realized what change in their relationship that would require.

How long? he wondered. How many months or even years would it take before they might reach that level of mutual affection and understanding? How long—if ever— before she would not think of her first husband and the love they had shared? William felt instantly guilty for even having such a thought. Was it even right of him to hope such a thing? Especially when his marriage to Charlotte had so clearly been a business transaction of mutual benefit for both. A few days ago he would not have believed he would be considering such matters, but somehow his feelings for her were much more than he had anticipated.

Sometime during his musings, she had opened her eyes and now lay smiling up at him.

"Come join us." She reached across Alec to pat the bed on the other side of him.

William hesitated, feeling that perhaps even this was too intimate a situation for them just yet.

We are *married,* he reminded himself. *And there will be a child between us.*

Wordlessly, he removed his shoes, then crossed the room to the bed. Carefully, so as not to wake Alec, he lay on the bed beside him, facing Charlotte.

They each lifted a hand at the same moment, and after a brief hesitation she reached for his. William entwined their fingers, enjoying her touch once more.

"Is this how you sleep each night?" he asked, hugging

the edge of the mattress. "I can't imagine that it makes for a very good rest."

"Sometimes it doesn't." She smiled. "Alec does not lie this still very long. Sometime in the night he will begin to roll and squirm."

"But I can see how it is nice to spend some quiet time with him when he is so serene—and smells rather good." William inhaled deeply, breathing in the baby sweet scent.

"He has just had a bath," Charlotte said. "But come back in the morning. He often does not smell so sweet then."

William chuckled softly at this. "He needs his own bed," he said. "And you need yours. There is a fine, large room that would suit you both. It is in the far wing . . . next to mine." He let the suggestion hang in the air, more than curious as to how she would take it.

"If you are offering, I would like that," Charlotte said.

He would like that too, he decided, having her closer, even when they slept. The room beside his would do nicely. And in his mind, it was a positive step forward in the direction of their marriage.

CHAPTER

December 23

At breakfast Charlotte was disappointed to find only one place setting and an envelope bearing her name beside it. After being seated she opened it quickly to find an apology from William, stating that he had urgent business and would be away most of the day.

Disappointment surged through her. She had become used to his company. *As I should not,* she told herself. At the new year, he would return to the normality of his life and running his business, and she would be left by herself—save for the servants—to decipher what her purpose and routine should be.

There was caring for Alec, of course, but without other chores and responsibilities to occupy her time, Charlotte knew there would be far too many free hours. *Which will never do.* She would have to find something else to keep her busy. *For starters, I shall have to make this house my home.*

She would begin this morning by moving her

belongings into the room beside William's in the east wing, as he had suggested she might do.

After a hurried breakfast—dining alone was not enjoyable—she made arrangements for Alec's continued care, then went in search of Mrs. Duff to make her request.

"Mr. Vancer said you might inquire about that today," Mrs. Duff said. "I could tell that he hoped you would," she said to Charlotte as an aside and with a knowing sort of sparkle in her eye.

"It was very kind of him to offer," Charlotte said, while a twinge of worry took hold in her heart. She followed Mrs. Duff to the aforementioned room and took a minute to look around while the housekeeper went to fetch help with moving Charlotte's belongings.

William had not been exaggerating when he'd said the room was larger. It was at least twice as big as the one she'd been staying in, with plenty of space to put an additional bed for Alec. A large window seat overlooked the front of the house, and a fine brick fireplace graced the opposite wall and boasted two comfortable looking chairs beside.

The bed was a tall four poster with a beautifully embroidered coverlet that looked as if it had never been used.

It hasn't, Charlotte realized. *This was intended to be Marsali's room. William wanted to marry Marsali. I am just a poor substitute.* Surely William had offered this room to her only as a kindness and because of Alec.

Still, the inkling of concern she'd felt increased when she noticed the door that stood between the bed and dressing table. After only a second's hesitation, Charlotte opened it and stared at the chamber on the other side. Her worry increased tenfold.

His room. Of course. William had told her as much. And she ought to have known there would be a connecting door. She'd seen the same in some of the houses she'd cleaned. It was not uncommon.

But the marriage we have is not common. It was not a real marriage, in the sense that most were. That hers and Matthew's had been. *It is a marriage of convenience, a business arrangement.*

But standing in the doorway, staring at the bed William slept on, she did not feel very businesslike at all. On impulse, she stepped into his room. His dinner jacket from the previous evening lay draped over the chair. Out of habit, from years of servitude, she picked it up, intending to place it in his dressing room. But his familiar scent clung to it, catching her off guard, sending her senses and emotions temporarily reeling.

Charlotte closed her eyes and clutched the jacket to her chest as a dozen images from the past few days scrolled through her mind. William looking so vulnerable on the church steps as he asked her if she was certain she wished to marry him. William wiping snow from his face. William hoisting Alec on his shoulders so he might see the ships better. William lying beside them in bed last night.

She dropped the jacket and fled the room, closing the connecting door and locking it securely. She only just resisted the urge to move the bureau in front of it. *As if that will stop this madness.*

It could be nothing else, this thinking of her new husband in any other terms but as an amiable partner. Someday, perhaps, she might feel differently. *But not now.* Not with Matthew so recently gone and this marriage so new.

Forgive me, Matthew. But she did not even know what

she was asking forgiveness for this time. And she dared not ponder it to find out.

After a busy morning spent relocating her belongings to the new room and playing with Alec, Charlotte had enjoyed both her larger fireplace and the window seat, indulging in an afternoon of reading while Alec napped, all the while keeping half an eye on the comings and goings in the street below.

It was dark and would soon be time to dress for dinner. William had not returned home, and she was starting to worry. No one in the house knew his whereabouts—or they were not telling Charlotte if they did. Feeling something between irritation and concern, she pressed her face to the window looking down on Fifth Street.

A wagon was approaching, bringing a delivery of some sort, no doubt. The residents in this neighborhood did not drive wagons, that she could tell, but instead all owned fine carriages kept in carriage houses behind the main buildings.

She followed the wagon's progress up the street and was surprised when it stopped in front of the house. Even more surprising was that William himself jumped down from the seat. She watched as he paid the driver then went around back to heft an enormous fir tree from the wagon bed.

A Christmas tree!

Charlotte flew from the room, scarcely remembering to close the door behind her, lest Alec wake. She ran down the stairs and arrived breathless at the front door, in time to beat the butler to his post and open it herself.

"You've brought us a Christmas tree! Oh, thank you." Impulsively she threw her arms around William's neck as he struggled to bring the tree inside.

"Charlotte," he choked. She released him and stepped back, laughing.

Moving behind him, she attempted to lift the top of the tree and keep it from dragging across the floor. A trail of pine needles followed their progress from the foyer to the parlor, and her fingers were soon sticky with sap. At last William set the great tree down and paused to wipe his sleeve across his forehead.

"Oh, thank you," Charlotte said once more, though this time she refrained from hugging him. "Our father always brought us a Christmas tree, and I haven't had one in years—not since we left France."

"I know." In spite of his evident fatigue, he grinned. "Marsali told me all about the trees your family had. I realized this morning that we had no Christmas for Alec. So I set about remedying that as quickly as possible." He inclined his head toward the hall, where servants laden with packages were making their way in.

"Goodness," Charlotte exclaimed. "Whatever have you bought?"

"Things little boys need—from new mittens and knickers to blocks and a rocking horse. This shall be a Christmas to remember."

Charlotte hugged herself to keep from throwing her arms around William once more and burying her face in his neck and bursting into tears. "How—" She turned away, waving a hand in front of her face, as if that would somehow ward off the moisture spilling from her eyes.

"What is it? What is wrong?" William was beside her at once, his hands on her shoulders, and he turned her gently to face him.

"Nothing is wrong. Everything is *right*," Charlotte said, realizing she made no sense at all. *Too right*. "Only how am I supposed to repay you when you are always doing kindness after kindness for us? You have everything to give, and I have nothing."

He walked to the parlor doors and shut them, then gathered her in his arms, where she cried, as she had feared she would.

"You gave me everything when you married me," William insisted a few minutes later when her tears were spent. He led them both to the settee.

"You saved Vancer Furs. Without a wife, I would have lost an important inheritance—one that is already financing expansion to the west—something I must do if I wish to remain in competition with both Astor and Hyde."

"But that didn't cost me anything," she sniffled. "It was easy."

"Was it?" He took her hand in his, caressing the back of it with his thumb. "I believe it cost you plenty to say 'I do,' a second time—to a man you don't love and barely know."

"You mustn't say that." She lifted her tear-stained face to his. "I *do* know you. A better man I could not have found, and I—"

"Careful," he advised, stopping her. "Don't say anything that you will regret later—anything you are not sure of. Honesty between us is all that I require now. I would not wish to hear something that isn't truthful."

He was right, of course. Charlotte pressed her lips together, to keep them from speaking the thoughts swirling through her mind. She loved Matthew. Always, she would love Matthew, and she never wanted that to change, did she?

She and William had something different—a mutual friendship and respect, and she needed to be content with that. Marrying each other had not been a first choice for either; that it was working out so well needn't alter anything else—past or future.

She swallowed the regret that came with these sensible thoughts and tugged her hand carefully from his.

With a smile she did not quite feel, she clasped her hands together and stood, determined to be content and grateful for all she had.

CHAPTER

December 24

"It is the loveliest tree I have ever seen," Charlotte exclaimed for at least the tenth time as she stood back to admire their handiwork. During the afternoon hours, she and William had been busy tying ribbons and carefully placing candles—from one of the many boxes he'd brought home yesterday—upon the tree.

The fresh pine scent engulfed the room, and Charlotte felt that if she but closed her eyes she would find herself a little girl again, trudging with her father through the forest near their home in France as they searched for the perfect tree.

As if he'd read her mind, William promised, "Next year you and Alec can come with me to help find the tree. And we will plan ahead and make an outing of it, so it is not a before-dawn-until-dark expedition as was yesterday's."

Next year. "You cannot know how good it feels to hear

that," Charlotte said, bestowing a smile of gratitude upon him.

William chuckled. "If it means that much to you, perhaps we should get a tree for *every* holiday."

"I was not speaking of the tree." Charlotte clasped nervous hands in front of her, half-wishing she had contained her thoughts. But now that she had spoken she must explain herself. "Knowing that we shall still be here next Christmas, and the one beyond that and the one beyond that . . ." She turned away, walking to the window that overlooked the snowy yard. "It brings a great measure of comfort." She glanced over her shoulder at him. "That you have given us a home."

"You—and Matthew—did not reside in the same home throughout your marriage?" William came to stand beside her, close but not too much so. In the past few days they had been silently figuring out boundaries—what each might say and do that would not cross a line of discomfort for the other.

Charlotte shook her head. "We did not. Before we left England, we had saved enough for my passage, but Matthew traveled under indenture. His first employer in Virginia was a kind man. He allowed me to work for our lodging, while Matthew's labor went solely toward paying off his debt." She smiled wistfully. Those first two years had been good—or as good as they'd enjoyed. "Then the plantation was sold, and Matthew's indenture with it, and the next owner was not as sympathetic. I had to take work elsewhere and went to live with a different family. For a good year and a half, Matthew and I saw each other only on Sundays."

"And this was your circumstance when your husband died?"

"No." Charlotte turned away from the window and

faced William. She'd dreaded speaking to him of Matthew but found now that she had started, it was not as difficult as she had feared. In some ways, it felt a relief to tell him, to share with someone the sorrows that had been hers and hers alone for too long.

Marsali had been too consumed with her own grief to listen to Charlotte's tale. And before that . . . *No one to listen or care.* Matthew had not been the only man killed in the accident at the mill; the whole town had been consumed with grief, with none to spare for the newcomer's wife, especially considering the circumstances.

"Last April Matthew's passage was finally repaid. He found work at the mill in another town, and we were renting a small cabin. I planted a garden, and we were beginning to save money for our own farm." Charlotte closed her eyes briefly, as if to shut out the painful memories.

At a gentle pressure on her hands, she looked up and found William's gaze upon her.

"You don't have to tell me any more if you don't wish to."

"I know." She allowed him to lead her back to the settee, where they sat silently admiring the lovely tree. How had she allowed the mood to turn melancholy? She didn't want to feel this way, not now, not on Christmas Eve and when William had worked so hard to make the holiday special for Alec.

But *well begun is half done,* her mother used to say, and Charlotte did not wish to leave this half done. *Just tell him— all of it.*

"In late July there was an accident at the mill. Three men were killed. Matthew was seriously injured. Everyone said it was his fault. They brought him home to me, and I tried to take care of him. But his leg and chest had been crushed, and there was something inside hurting him, making him suffer terribly. I tried, but I couldn't help him. I couldn't ease his pain."

"Was there no physician summoned?" William asked, his face drawn and concern reflected in his own eyes.

"The doctor came—once," Charlotte said, reminding herself that being bitter helped no one. "His son was one of those killed, and it seemed to me as if he did not try very hard to help Matthew."

"How long did he suffer?" William asked quietly.

"Six days—nearly a whole week." How it hurt to think of that time—the worst six days of her life. At least after Matthew was gone, she'd known he wasn't in pain any longer. Seeing him suffer and being helpless to do anything about it, anything for him, had left her drained and hardly feeling alive herself. If not for Alec, she might not have been. "I never left his side, except to care for Alec. No one came to see how Matthew was. And after—no one bothered to see how Alec and I fared. I was carrying another baby but lost it in the two weeks after Matthew's death. After that I took Alec and returned to my previous employer. Without Matthew to help, and in my own, weakened condition, I couldn't make enough for room and board for Alec and me, let alone anything else we needed. I didn't know how we were going to get through the winter. When your carriage arrived, it seemed an answer to my desperate prayer."

"I remember making that decision," William said. "It happened at the oddest of times. I was at work, in the middle of writing up a contract for a new client, when the idea came that I should send for Marsali's sister. And so I stopped what I was doing and did so right then."

"Thank heaven," they both said at once, echoing the other's thoughts. Charlotte found that she could laugh, and the corner of William's eyes crinkled as he smiled at her.

"How old are you?" he asked when her mirth had fled.

"Twenty-four. And you?"

"Ten years your senior," he said soberly. "Yet your hardships have no doubt made you wiser than I."

"I am not certain 'wise' is the right word." She lay her head back against the sofa and was not entirely surprised to find William's arm behind her.

"They have made you gentle, then," William said.

"Grateful. Cautious."

He was correct on all counts, though she did not tell him so. She had known what it was to lose the man you loved, and so she had felt empathy for Marsali and treated her gently, as she had wished to be treated—and had not been—following Matthew's death.

And I am grateful to be here, to be warm and safe, to have food enough for Alec.

And cautious—who wouldn't be? Charlotte didn't know if she could ever live through pain as she'd felt last summer again. Keeping William at arm's length, not allowing herself to become too attached to him, was definitely the safer route.

And then there was guilt. She felt it constantly. Matthew had suffered and died from trying to provide for her. And she had repaid him by marrying another.

William's fingers brushed her shoulders, and Charlotte straightened quickly, scooting to the edge of the settee, though a part of her would have liked nothing more than to escape into the comfort of his arm around her.

A long, awkward minute passed in silence.

At length William spoke. "I will do my best to care for you as Matthew would have."

"Thank you," Charlotte murmured, not daring to say more. He was already caring for her too much, and would she but allow it, she feared William might do just as he said, caring for her as Matthew, and completely obscuring her memory of him in the process.

CHAPTER 10

December 25

William withdrew his pocket watch from his vest and glanced at it again. "Alec has been riding that horse for twenty-two minutes."

"I do believe you have hired your first nanny, one that will be quite good at keeping Alec occupied for great lengths of time." Charlotte sat on the floor beside Alec as he rocked, though she had quickly realized he had full command of the rocking horse and there was little cause for concern. At least with regard to injury. She feared a tantrum when she removed him from the toy at naptime.

"At this length he shall be five years old before we get to unwrapping the parcel with the blocks." William's tone was good natured as he tucked away his watch.

"He is obviously delighted with it," Charlotte said. "You have given him the perfect gift."

"Let us hope I am as successful with yours." William crossed the room to stand closer to them.

Guilt—for all he had done and was doing for her—rushed to the forefront of her mind. "You have already bought me gowns and hats and shoes and a new cloak this week." Charlotte looked up at him. "Please do not get me anything else. I feel badly enough that I am unable to give you even a simple gift."

William leaned close to her, one hand extended. Charlotte took it and allowed him to pull her to a standing position. "This gift is not something that I am purchasing for *you*."

"For Alec, then? But you have given him everything he could possibly need or want as well."

"Precisely," William said. "Plus, he is too little to understand, so this item is not for him either, though I do hope it will hold some importance for him as he grows older."

Charlotte felt her curiosity piqued. She tilted her head, looking up so she might meet William's eyes. It did not appear that he was teasing. "I give up then. I suppose I shall just have to wait until you give me this present that is not for me or Alec."

"You shall have to wait," William agreed mysteriously, then said no more on the matter. "Church services start on the hour. We should go soon if we wish to get a seat up front. I think Alec will enjoy it more if he can see all of the candles."

"Spoken like a father already," Charlotte said, feeling her heart expand a little more. She allowed William to help her with her cloak, all the while commanding her insides to quit fluttering at his touch as he lifted her hair and his hands brushed her shoulders. When she had fastened the clasp, he still stood behind her, and the urge to lean into him for just a moment became too much to resist. As she took the tiniest step back, his arms came around her, and he leaned close, his face near to hers.

No words were exchanged; none were needed as they stood together, watching Alec still rocking furiously before the glow of the Christmas tree.

"Perfect." William broke the silence with his whisper. Then with an audible sigh he released her and stepped back.

Charlotte felt the absence of his warmth and much more, but she dared not dwell on that.

"How are we ever to get him off of that thing?" she asked, looking down on Alec. "Or do you propose we take him to church on it?" She laughed at the foolishness of her own suggestion.

Instead of answering her, William withdrew a candy stick from his pocket and knelt beside Alec. Placing his hand on the back of the rocking horse, William gradually brought it to a stop.

"Would you like to go for a ride outside and have a piece of candy?" he asked.

"Candy," Alec repeated and held his hands out to William.

"You'll spoil him," Charlotte scolded half-heartedly.

"That is my intention." William scooped Alec into his arms. "Today, at least. And on his birthday, and when we picnic in the summer, and when he is old enough for a real horse and—"

Charlotte laughed. "I can see now the kind of father you are going to be."

Uncertainty filled William's gaze as he looked at her.

"A wonderful one," she finished, swallowing the emotion that had risen in her throat. The past five days had found her more wont to cry and laugh than she had for quite some time. *I was numb for so long,* Charlotte realized. She had coped by feeling nothing, and now it seemed that William was causing her to feel everything.

CHAPTER 11

December 28

illiam cradled a sleepy Alec in his arms as they left the church. Between his wedding, Christmas services, and the Sunday services today, it was the third time in a week he'd been to church, each time more favorable than the previous.

Because Charlotte is at my side. On the day of their wedding he had been too consumed with worry to enjoy much of anything until after the ceremony. Christmas services had been pleasant, until Charlotte had to take Alec out to tend to him before the meeting was over. But today Alec had slept through most of the bishop's message and the choir and congregation singing. William had offered to hold him, and Charlotte had happily agreed. For a toddler, Alec was already quite large, and no doubt her arms became tired.

For William the novelty of holding a sleeping child was a new and wonderful experience. *Innocence in my arms and perfection at my side.* After being in their presence for eight days, he'd come to think of Alec and Charlotte in those terms. Of course she was not truly perfect; no one was, though he'd yet to see many of her flaws. *She is perfect for me.* Marrying her was the best thing that had ever happened to him. He only wished he knew how to make her feel the same.

Charlotte walked ahead of him, pausing just outside the church under the shelter of its tall roof, looking lovelier than ever in a new outfit of deepest blue that had been delivered yesterday. Her expression was contemplative and serious, causing him to wonder—and worry—about the direction of her thoughts. Sometime during the service snow had begun falling again, so they took a minute to don their cloaks and coats and mittens and hats. In one arm he carried Alec down the steps, while his other hand held firmly to Charlotte's.

William could not bear the thought of anything—even something as little as a harmless fall—happening to either of them. *How much anguish Charlotte must have endured, watching her husband suffer.* William had thought on this many times since she had shared it with him. That Matthew's death still troubled her seemed a given. William only wished he knew how to lift such a burden from her.

With care he climbed into the carriage and sat beside her, leaving the seat across from them vacant. "Together we can keep Alec warm on the ride home," he said by way of explanation.

Charlotte nodded while biting her lip, giving William no doubt that she saw through his flimsy excuse for being so close to her.

"Look. Our snow angels are still there." She pointed out the window as they passed the park.

William smiled, recalling that enjoyable morning, remembering how he had first wanted to kiss her as she'd stood there, armed with snowballs, her cheeks rosy with cold. It was a desire he'd felt repeatedly over the last several days but had contented himself with holding her hand occasionally and sitting near her when they were together.

"I wonder how Marsali is faring," Charlotte said, leaning her head against the seat. Her thoughts obviously lay a different direction from his.

"Marsali is well, I hope," William said. "I expect we shall hear from her when she has found Mr. Thatcher. I expect Lady Cosgrove will return to us then also." He found that he no longer harbored ill feelings toward the woman. After all, it was she who had suggested that Charlotte take Marsali's place.

"Are you the least sorry that Christopher . . ." Charlotte's voice trailed off, and she looked out her window, away from him.

"Am I the least sorry that Marsali's husband is alive? No. Not at all." He felt discomfited to realize he would have felt vastly different had he learned that Charlotte's husband had somehow returned from the dead.

"Are *you* sorry?" William asked, suddenly worried that was what this line of questioning was leading to. That Charlotte felt regret for marrying him.

"No." She turned to him, placing a gentle hand on his, as was her custom when she was in earnest about something. It was one of her many little traits he adored already. "I am most happy for Marsali and most grateful to be married to you."

Grateful. There was that word again. Charlotte used it daily, and if William could find fault in her for one thing, that was it. He appreciated her gratitude but yearned to be the cause of her feeling something more. He reminded himself again of her loss, of the wounds that still likely ran deep and had to be healing. *Patience,* he admonished himself. He hadn't planned to want more from their marriage and to want it so soon. Certainly he could not expect her feelings to match his. But he wanted them to.

What will it take to get her to feel something other than gratitude toward me?

The folded paper held nervously in his hands, William approached Charlotte where she sat by the fire in the parlor, a forgotten book in her lap as she stared, apparently lost in thought, at the embers burning low in the grate.

"I was wondering if you would like your present now?" he asked.

She smiled as she looked up at him. "Doesn't a woman always like presents?"

It wasn't the answer he had expected, and he felt glad of it. That she had not started off with the list of things he had already done for her seemed a good sign. He had not intended to tell her what he had done so soon, but rather to take her to see it sometime after Marsali was settled and she and her sister might visit. But William had found that he wished to tell Charlotte now of the action he had taken. He sensed there was more on the subject of Charlotte's husband that needed to be shared between them before they might move forward, and if they did not discuss it before he returned to work, who knew when the opportunity would present itself?

She had shared with him much on Christmas Eve, concluding with the fact that Matthew had nothing to mark his grave, in a lone corner of a small churchyard. William had determined to fix that, to put Charlotte's mind at ease regarding her first husband, insomuch as he could.

"I had planned to show you in person, but with the weather as it is, that might be months away. And I thought this might bring you a measure of peace." He held the letter out to her. It had arrived this evening, along with the servant he had dispatched to accomplish the errand in the first place.

Charlotte straightened in her seat and took the paper from him. She unfolded it and began to read aloud.

> *Dear Mr. Vancer,*
>
> *As per your request, a headstone bearing the inscription* Matthew Holbrook, loving husband and father, *was fashioned from our finest granite and placed as directed. Please inform us if we may be of further service.*
>
> *Sincerely,*
> *Robert Keeler, Mason*

"I didn't know the dates to put on it, but Mr. Keeler said those could be added later." William shoved his hands in his pockets and tried to appear nonchalant as he awaited Charlotte's reaction.

She read the letter once more, to herself this time, as if she did not quite understand or believe its contents. When at last she looked up at him, her eyes glistened with unshed tears. "I don't understand. Why would you go to the trouble to do this? You didn't even know Matthew."

"But you did." William ventured closer, taking the chair opposite her and scooting it near to hers. "This was important to you. And I hoped it might bring you some measure of peace—a sense of closure." He winced inwardly, realizing how selfish the latter sounded. Likely one could never have closure when a spouse died.

Charlotte refolded the paper carefully and placed it in her lap. "This was exceedingly kind and thoughtful. Thank you, William." She did not look up at him but kept her gaze downcast and took a deep breath, alerting William that she was not finished speaking and that there was a good chance he would not care for what she had to say.

"I will always love Matthew. I must." Charlotte twisted the silver band on her finger. When William had asked her if she wished to continue to wear her other wedding ring also, she had told him she'd never had one. They had been too poor. "To do anything less would seem wrong."

"I understand." William stood abruptly, unable or unwilling to hear the rest of her explanation or rejection. *Perhaps someday . . .* But certainly not now. He could not expect her affection to turn toward him as quickly as his had turned to her. He was going to have to extend his patience far beyond these twelve days in December. He must remember that he had achieved the purpose of his marriage. *Because of her, my business is saved.* But somehow that seemed to matter little right now. Running Vancer Furs did not hold the appeal it had before his marriage.

"Goodnight, Charlotte. Sleep well." He left the room before she could say more, hurrying to his own, where he lay awake for quite some time, staring at the door separating them. When he was finally nearing sleep, the sound of weeping woke him again. William climbed out of bed and stood near the door, even going so far as to try the knob. He was not surprised to find it locked. Feeling helpless, he stood in the dark, listening to his wife cry out her sorrows in the room beyond.

He hung his head, wondering how he could have been so wrong in the selection of his gift and in believing—even for a few days—that Charlotte was feeling the same attraction he was and that their marriage would become something far more than either had hoped for.

How he wished he hadn't been mistaken.

CHAPTER 12

December 29

Charlotte thanked her dance partner and returned to the side of the Fredericses' ballroom, where she attempted to blend into the crowd and stand inconspicuously, waiting and hoping for William to join her.

As with the balls in England, she had discovered that there were rules in America as well, one of them apparently being that a husband and wife rarely saw one another when attending a ball together. The night was nearly over—thank goodness—and Charlotte had yet to dance with William once. Rarely had she been at his side either, as Mrs. Frederick had whisked her away from the moment of their arrival and had been busy introducing Charlotte to one person after another all evening.

Seeing their hostess coming her way yet again, Charlotte stepped behind a group of gentlemen, then ducked around the corner and into the hall, away from the stuffy ballroom.

A curtained alcove to the side beckoned her, and

Charlotte stepped into it and was relieved to discover it empty. She sank into the nearest chair and kicked off her slippers, bringing blessed relief to feet unaccustomed to dancing the night away.

At breakfast, when William had first tentatively reminded her that they were to attend the Frederickses' ball this evening, Charlotte had fretted over what an evening of dancing with him would do to her fragile resolve. The previous evening, when he had presented his gift, showing her the receipt for Matthew's headstone, Charlotte had feared she might kiss him, she was so overcome. She had started to explain herself, to share her theory on different kinds of love. But William had not stayed to hear it, rushing off to bed, leaving Charlotte knowing she had disappointed him.

Feeling as if she was the most wretched woman ever to have lived—for being unfaithful to Matthew and unloving to William—Charlotte had spent a long night crying herself to sleep.

Voices sounded outside the alcove, so Charlotte stood, prepared to leave if her place of respite was discovered.

"He's even more pathetic than when we were engaged," a female voice announced. "I heard he had to practically beg the woman to marry him—and she's not even from our circles."

"I heard she's a widow," another female voice said.

The first spoke again. "I heard that too. And she has a child. William Vancer couldn't even find a woman who hadn't been married already." A fit of giggles followed.

Charlotte held her breath and took a step back, lest the curtain rustle and she be revealed. Who were these women, and why were they speaking so unkindly of William?

"Well, one thing is certain. He doesn't love her. *I* broke

his heart when I eloped with Avery the day William and I were to be married, and it will take more than some widowed farm girl for him to forget that day, and to forget me."

"That he has married suggests that he has, dear," a third voice chimed in.

"That's what you think," the first woman said. "Would you care for a small wager on the matter? The men needn't have all the fun gaming."

"I don't know, Daphne. I've seen William Vancer when he's angry, and he isn't one you wish to cross."

"Anger is not the emotion I plan to illicit from him." The woman who had to be Daphne laughed. "Come along, girls, and I will prove to you that I've ruined Mr. Vancer for any woman who might set her cap for him—including that mousey wife of his."

There was murmured agreement to this, and the group moved off. Charlotte peeked through the curtain as soon as she dared and caught a glimpse of a yellow gown before it disappeared around the corner into the ballroom.

Bringing a hand to her head, she leaned against the wall. *William was engaged to be married before—before Marsali and Lydia.* He had not spoken of it, and little wonder, given the sound of the abuses he had suffered at this woman's—at Daphne's—hand.

"I broke his heart . . ." Why would someone boast of such an act? Charlotte felt a surge of protective anger. *William is out there—with that woman, who intends to hurt him again.*

I will not let her. Jamming her sore feet into her slippers, she decided what she must do. She left the alcove but, instead of returning to the ballroom, hurried up the stairs to the hall above. Once there, she looked down upon the occupants of the ballroom until she located her husband, speaking with a group of men.

Still safe, then.

Charlotte did not bother searching for the woman in the yellow gown but instead flew down the staircase and crossed the ballroom to stand at William's side. He was still conversing with two men she had been introduced to on their wedding day and again this evening, Lord Thornthrope and Mr. Astor. Charlotte placed her hand upon William's arm and waited, not so patiently, for him to finish speaking.

With the first lull in conversation, he looked at her, surprise registering on his face. Worry must have shown on hers.

"Are you all right? Has something happened?"

"Not at all." *Not yet, anyway.* She forced a smile. "I have missed your company this evening is all."

"It's a rare woman who says that to her husband," Lord Thornthrope said jovially.

"Good for you, Vancer, for finding yourself a wife who cares for more than your pocketbook," Mr. Astor said.

"I have been most fortunate," William said, bestowing a look of such tender affection upon her that Charlotte felt her confidence boosted in what she was about to ask of him. There might not be love between them, but there was respect and friendship and a strong attraction, and perhaps that would be enough—for a few minutes, at least—to pretend something more.

"The night grows late, and we have yet to dance," Charlotte said.

William's mouth lifted in a smile. "A situation we must remedy at once." He gave a slight bow to their companions. "If you will excuse us, gentlemen."

Charlotte curtsied to them. "Good eve. It was a pleasure to see you again." They offered similar sentiments, then stepped aside, allowing William to lead her toward the center of the floor, where couples were taking their places for the next waltz. Charlotte leaned in close to him as they walked. Lowering her voice to a whisper, she pled, "I have a favor to request."

"Anything." He paused, glancing at her with concern. "What is it you wish?"

"Please dance with me . . . as if you are in love with me." The words sounded needy and desperate, but Charlotte could take no thought for her own pride at this moment—only his was at stake. She must show that Daphne woman that she had not crushed William, that he had moved beyond the hurt she had caused him.

That he is so much better than she.

William's brows drew together with concern, and he reached his hand up to cover hers on his arm. "I care a great deal for you, Charlotte."

"I know." She spoke hastily and as quiet as possible. "I will explain later. Just please. Pretend feelings beyond our friendship—for this one dance, I beg of you."

"You need not beg." The tension between his brow ceased, and his gaze upon her turned tender once more. He brushed a straying hair from her face and allowed his hand to linger. "Only know this. I am not good at pretending, so do not mistake my actions for that. As I told you once before, when I begin something, I never change course. What I start in this moment, with this dance, is irrevocable."

Charlotte felt herself nodding slowly, so as not to break their gaze or to entirely give her word that she was in agreement or understood. *Pretending to love me is irrevocable or . . .* The other possibility was too frightening. *Ours is a marriage of convenience.* She'd been telling herself that for nine days now and believing it less and less.

But she had reconciled her mind and heart to that course. To venture into deeper feelings would require further emotional distance from Matthew. He could not be her last thought at night if she allowed herself to love William. Already she struggled with that, with remembering Matthew often enough and the feelings she had for him. *But it will become easier again, when our twelve days in December are over.* William would return to spending his days at work, and she would settle into the routine of being mistress of his house, drawing on different memories—those of her mother when Charlotte was but a girl and living on a grand estate in France.

Friendship, nothing more. But for this one dance, for the remainder of the night, she must pretend otherwise.

During her musings, William had guided them to take their places for the waltz. He faced her. "Of a sudden you have grown quite serious. Do you wish to recant your request?"

"Not at all." She gave him what she hoped was a coy look, peering up through her eyelashes. She should not have become discomfited by his words. That was all they were—words. And this was all pretending, and she must do it well. She cared for him and could not bear the things she'd heard Daphne say of him.

Recalling those, and how much gratitude she felt to William for literally rescuing her and Alec, Charlotte placed her hand on his shoulder and lifted her head to meet his gaze. His eyes held no amusement, but rather a new intensity she had not witnessed before.

His hand came to her waist, pulling her in closer than necessary, or perhaps decent. His other hand claimed hers, but not before he brought it to his lips for a lingering kiss.

The first strains of music began, and William stepped forward and was soon leading her in flawless circles about the room. She wasn't certain how he could guide them so skillfully, as his gaze never left hers to look elsewhere and judge where they might be going or the distance between other couples. Charlotte found herself unable to look away. The blue of his eyes seemed to deepen as they regarded her in a way they had not before.

"You look beautiful tonight." His gaze at last left her own to drop to her lips.

"Thank you." She sounded and felt breathless, though the dance was not taxing. "It is all I can do to appear fine enough to stand at the side of my handsome husband."

A corner of his mouth lifted. "Do you know that I cannot recall a time—before now—when someone told me that I am handsome?"

"Well, you are." Charlotte tucked that information away, telling herself she must remember to compliment him often.

"Then we are both fortunate, indeed, as will our children be."

He squeezed her hand as he said this, both his action and words causing her heart to pound. Of course he would want children of his own. She'd known that when she agreed to marry him. But she had also believed it would be some time—*years?*—before either felt comfortable enough to broach that subject. What had she done in asking him to pretend love?

From the corner of her eye, Charlotte caught a flash of yellow.

She longed to look and see the face of the person attached to it but dared not. Neither did she need to, in order to confirm her suspicions. In the second she had been distracted, William's face had paled. His jaw clenched tight, and his grip on her hand became almost painful.

It is she. This woman who hurt him.

Desperate to distract him, to save him further pain, Charlotte returned to the subject at hand. "William, how many children would you like?"

"How many—" His gaze snapped back to her.

"Yes." She took a deep breath and plunged on. "The farming families where I lived in Virginia had quite a number of children—some as many as a dozen. But I imagine that here in the city it is different."

"I don't really know," he admitted. "I have not paid attention to such things, nor thought on them much myself."

That was reassuring, at least. "But you would—like a child of your own. At least one." She could not quite believe they were having this conversation *here* in the middle of a crowded ballroom, just days after they had wed. But she could think of nothing else that might distract him enough.

She dared a glance to her left and caught the woman in the yellow dress staring at them. Charlotte turned quickly back to William and found him watching her, a look of sudden understanding dawning.

He drew her closer yet and bent to whisper in her ear. "I would like a child, Charlotte. *Our* child. No one else's. Certainly not Daphne Hyde's." He circled them away, maneuvering, Charlotte suspected, to get them farther from his former fiancée.

"However," he continued, his face close to hers once more. "All in good time. I find that I should very much like to kiss you first." Upon saying this he drew back, as if to gauge her reaction.

Though she'd believed herself beyond blushing, Charlotte felt her cheeks heating. And she could not seem to keep her eyes from William's mouth, from those inviting lips that were smiling at her in a knowing sort of way.

She felt suddenly grateful for the pressure of his hand at her back, and for the strength of his arm supporting hers midair, for she felt weak and unable to think clearly.

Looking into his eyes once more, a rush of emotion that had nothing to do with gratitude crashed over her. This man she was dancing with, this intelligent, kind, handsome man, was hers. Surely he could have had his choice of many women, yet somehow it was she who had the good fortune to be here in his arms. *To be his wife. To someday carry his child.*

She felt dizzy and overly warm and delightfully giddy all at once, as if she'd just awoken and realized where she was and who she was with. *He is mine. I am his.* It was more than the sense of security she had craved, more than the friendship that had grown in the past days. *Frighteningly more.* She felt like a schoolgirl again and, had she only closed her eyes, might have believed she was back in England, a seventeen-year-old girl dancing with a man for the very first time.

Instead of closing, her eyes opened wide as she recognized the feelings, the intensity she had not felt for so very long. *Matthew, forgive me.* But it was a half-hearted prayer. Her thoughts were all for the man before her. The one whose gaze spoke of longing and need and . . . love.

"There was no need to ask me to pretend," he whispered as their dance came to a close. "I am enchanted by you, and more than that, am coming to love you more rapidly than I ever would have believed possible. *You, Charlotte,* are the miracle of my life."

"I have thought of you the same way," she admitted. Only now it was a different sort of wonder she felt taking place. "Oh, William." She lay her head against his shoulder, heedless of what others around them might think.

He tucked his head close to hers. "I think I have had enough dancing for tonight. Let us go home."

CHAPTER 13

December 30

Charlotte woke the next day to find that Lady Cosgrove had returned, after seeing Marsali safely installed at Charlotte's previous place of employment. Charlotte was sad to learn that Christopher had not yet been located, and she spent a moment of worry, wondering what would happen should he not be found.

William spoke up from across the breakfast table. "We must continue to pray for them both, that they will find each other and be as happy as we are." He exchanged a look with Charlotte, as if to remind her of the barriers they had crossed last night. He had not kissed her, as he had said that he wanted to, but she knew it was only a matter of time before he did.

Before I truly betray Matthew. When dancing with William last night her path had seemed so clear. They were married, and she cared for him. What was wrong with allowing their feelings to progress? But with the rising of the sun and the snuggly little boy who more and more resembled his father, Charlotte had felt herself sinking into the despair of turmoil once more. How was she ever to be faithful to both Matthew and William?

Lady Cosgrove remained mostly silent during this exchange and the duration of breakfast, but shortly afterward, she visited Charlotte in her room.

"You do realize what you have been given, don't you?" Lady Cosgrove marched past Charlotte, still standing in the doorway, and sat in one of the chairs before the fire.

"Yes." Charlotte closed the door. "I do recognize that I am most fortunate to be here—to be married to William, to have my child and myself provided for. To attend balls and dinners, to dress in fine clothes and live in a grand house. I have lived without all of that, so I do understand its worth."

Lady Cosgrove clucked her tongue. "I was not speaking of those things. They are all well and good, and believe me, I enjoy them. But I was speaking of your husband—of Mr. Vancer and the way he cares for you. To love and be loved is the greatest blessing."

"Coming from one who tried to deprive two people of that very blessing, I find your sentiment somewhat unbelievable." Charlotte still could not forget the hurt done to Marsali; neither had she forgotten the way Lady Cosgrove had offered Charlotte herself up as a bride, without even consulting her first.

"Bah." Lady Cosgrove waved a hand in front of her face. "I did not believe Marsali and Mr. Thatcher were truly *in* love. They had known each other such a short time."

Not that short. Charlotte set about picking up Alec's blocks. He would return from breakfast soon, and then the blocks would be scattered about the room once more; but until then, they provided her with something to do.

"Mr. Vancer has fallen in love with you," Lady Cosgrove said. "And it is plain to see that you love him as well."

"I don't," Charlotte refuted swiftly. Then more softly, "I can't."

"Why not?" Lady Cosgrove demanded.

Charlotte changed topics. "Did you know William had been betrothed to someone before Lydia?

"You mean that woman in England?" Lady Cosgrove did not seem the least concerned.

England? "No. She is here," Charlotte said. "Last night I overheard her bragging about eloping with another man the day she was to marry William."

"Astonishing," Lady Cosgrove murmured. "I had no idea. I knew that he had been betrothed some years ago, when he was still living in England. They planned to marry and immigrate to America." She turned in her chair to better see Charlotte. "I don't know how much William has told you about his family, but he is the fifth son of a baron—and as such stood to inherit very little and had limited choices for employment. He was not content with this lot and so had saved up to pay for both his passage and his fiancée's. Then came the day they were to marry and sail to America, and she changed her mind. He went alone."

Charlotte placed the last of the blocks in the crate where they belonged, then sat on the bed and leaned forward, resting her chin on her hands. "Then that means that four times he has lost a fiancée—for one reason or another." *No wonder he acted as if he expected me to change my mind about marrying him.*

"I am glad you were not the fifth." Lady Cosgrove stood

abruptly. "I am fond of William. Our families go back a long time. He is a good man, and I should like to see him happy."

"I am doing my best," Charlotte said.

Lady Cosgrove crossed to the door but did not open it. "You are not doing any such thing but are holding yourself back from him."

"Of necessity," Charlotte insisted. "I *do* care for him."

"Then show it," Lady Cosgrove snapped. "Let your dead husband rest in peace, and honor his name and memory by loving again."

Charlotte lifted her head. "It is not so simple."

"I know it isn't." Lady Cosgrove's tone softened. "But easier for you than Mr. Vancer. He is the one who has been continuously rejected. You, on the other hand, were blessed with a loving relationship."

"Precisely what makes this so hard," Charlotte insisted.

"Not so." Lady Cosgrove shook a finger at her. "Think of how you loved your first husband. Had something happened to you, would you want him to be alone—to raise your son alone—the rest of his life?"

"Of course not." It would have been impossible for Matthew to care for Alec and work every day at the mill. And who would have cooked for them, washed their laundry . . . *cared for and loved them?* Charlotte swallowed uncomfortably.

"Mmm. Hmm." Lady Cosgrove nodded her head, as if following Charlotte's thoughts. "Can you honestly believe that *he* would want you to be alone? Or would he wish you to be cared for, happy—loved?"

"I don't know," Charlotte lied. She knew Matthew better than that, knew how selfless he'd been and that, no matter what, he would want the best for them, for she and Alec.

"It's a hard thing asked of us. I've been where you are,

and I remember," Lady Cosgrove said kindly. "But I also know that having loved before, you can again. Look to the future, Charlotte and the gift that has been given you."

CHAPTER 14

December 31

heir magical twelve days were over. It was time for William to return to work, to refocus his efforts on expanding Vancer Furs, to get back into his normal routine.

Three things he had no interest in or intention of doing—at least not as they had been done before.

"Checkmate." Instead of sounding smug that she had beaten him for the third time in as many days, Charlotte somehow managed to sound humble. "Thank you for the game. You are improving quite rapidly."

"Having someone to play with makes quite a difference in that." William stood, then walked around the table to assist Charlotte. But instead of pulling her chair out right away, he placed his hands on her shoulders and began rubbing gently. After a few minutes he felt her body relax. "That's better," he murmured.

He pulled the chair out and helped her up but did not

release her hand, leading her with him over to the picture window. Snow was falling again, huge white flakes twinkling in the lamplight outside.

"It's beautiful," she whispered.

He found the lowered volume of her voice telling and put his arms around her, while encouraging her to lean into him as she had once before. This time she did not hesitate, but complied at once, sighing as she did.

"What was that for?" he asked. Not a sigh of frustration or resignation or despair, he hoped.

"It was a sigh of contentment," Charlotte said. "I am perfectly happy and content with my life."

Also not what he wanted to hear. "Don't you ever want—more?" he asked boldly.

"Only since the night we danced."

It took him a second to register her response and what appeared to be a confession. He placed his hands on her shoulders and turned her around, so he might look into her eyes.

"Charlotte—"

"You have been so patient, William."

"I have not," he said.

"All right, you have not." They laughed together.

"How were we to know?" he asked her, continuing their dance of words around the unspoken topic of their deepening feelings for one another. *Our love.*

"We weren't." Charlotte placed her hands on the front of his shirt. "Miracles are like that, I suppose."

He prayed he was reading her right. "I don't want to take anything away from your past." *But I want you to be my future.*

"You won't." She smiled, and he recognized the look of serenity that he had glimpsed in her the morning they were married. "I know that now. Matthew first taught me how to love, but you have reminded me where to find it." Her hand slid to cover his heart.

"I have found myself in you, my purpose." William bent his head closer to hers as she raised up on her tiptoes.

"We both have." Those were the last of her whispered words before his lips covered hers in a meeting of sweetest caring and newly awakened passion. A minute later, when he pulled back to look at her, he was dismayed to find tears hovering in the corners of her eyes.

"Please don't cry. I'll stop," he promised, though he felt it might kill him to do so, to leave her and go off to his bed alone.

"Oh no you won't." She scrunched her fingers around the fabric of his shirt and pulled him closer again. "Just as I promise to never leave and to never stop loving you."

William's heart raced. He had told her once—just days earlier—not to speak of such emotion unless she meant it. The tender look in her eyes was not one of gratitude, but finally of something deeper, of commitment yes, but more than that he read desire and longing and joy in their depths, and it filled his soul with hope.

Behind them the clock struck midnight, ushering in the New Year. William saw to it that they kissed for the duration of the chimes.

Charlotte's cheeks were pink and her lips plump when he finally drew back. "Happy New Year, Mrs. Vancer. My love."

"For it to be as happy as possible—" Charlotte paused, a mischievous smile curving her lips. "I believe you should take some time off from work. What would you say to fifteen days—in January?"

More Hearthfire Romances

A Final Note

Thank you for reading *Twelve Days in December*, a companion novella in the Hearthfire Historical Romance series. The next novel in this line is set in Scotland during the late 1700s and revolves around the lives of twin brothers who are facing the difficulties of the Highland Clearances following the failed Jacobite uprising of 1745. Watch for previews and teasers on my website in coming months.

New this month, also from Mirror Press, is the *Timeless Regency Collection: A Midwinter Ball*. This volume features three novellas by three authors—Annette Lyon, Heidi Ashworth, and myself—all centered around a midwinter ball. I am equally excited to be one of the twelve authors involved in the Matchmaker series. Watch for the prequel novella this November and the twelve full-length romance novels to follow, one each month in 2016.

So many wonderful things to look forward to! Thank you for being a part of those. I continue to appreciate those who take the time to read my stories and those who post reviews as well. You make it possible for me to continue doing what I love.

If you would like more information about my other books and future releases, please visit MichelePaigeHolmes.com.

You can also follow me on Twitter at @MichelePHolmes.

Happy reading!
Michele

About Michele Paige Holmes

Michele Paige Holmes spent her childhood and youth in Arizona and northern California, often curled up with a good book instead of out enjoying the sunshine. She graduated from Brigham Young University with a degree in elementary education and found it an excellent major with which to indulge her love of children's literature.

Her first novel, *Counting Stars*, won the 2007 Whitney Award for Best Romance. Its companion novel, a romantic suspense titled *All the Stars in Heaven*, was a Whitney Award finalist, as was her first historical romance, *Captive Heart*. *My Lucky Stars* completed the Stars series.

In 2014 Michele launched the Hearthfire Historical Romance line, with the debut title, *Saving Grace*. *Loving Helen* is the companion novel, with a third, *Marrying Christopher* released in July 2015.

When not reading or writing romance, Michele is busy with her full-time job as a wife and mother. She and her husband live in Utah with their five high-maintenance children, and a Shitzu that resembles a teddy bear, in a house with a wonderful view of the mountains.

You can find Michele on the web:
MichelePaigeHolmes.com
Facebook: Michele Holmes
Twitter: @MichelePHolmes

Made in the USA
Las Vegas, NV
21 December 2020